A QUESTIONABLE
FRIENDSHIP

Cover Design by Scarlett Rugers

A QUESTIONABLE FRIENDSHIP

ISBN: 978-0-9911620-2-4

A QUESTIONABLE
FRIENDSHIP

A Novel

SAMANTHA MARCH

To my husband. I play for keeps.

PROLOGUE

September

"Brynne? It's time for you."

I moved my head just inches to the left, indicating I had heard my mother. I stared into the mirror, taking in my black dress with a hint of a bubble skirt, the string of pearls around my neck, and my red lips. Portland was always going on about the importance of lipstick, though I hardly ever wore any.

"Brynne? Everyone is waiting." I finally turned away from my reflection, meeting my mother's eyes. She squeezed my hand and slipped the index card with my speech on it into my sweaty palm. "You'll be just fine, darling. You can do it."

I nodded, feeling my brown bob graze my neck and then brush away. I walked out of the small room with my mom, entering the large area where everyone awaited my speech. I took my place, my hand shaking as I looked at the index card. I looked out over the sea of people, everyone from our small town there supporting Portland. I looked at my best friend next, taking in her shiny blonde hair, her smooth skin that never seemed to find a blemish or a sunburn, even when we stayed on the beach for hours. Her white dress didn't clash with her fair skin or light hair, it just made her look like she was glowing.

I cleared my throat. "Portland Dolish is my best friend." I looked over at her once more, tears filling my eyes. I paused before I could continue, and wrapped up just after a few minutes of speaking. I had agonized on my speech just nights before, reading and re-reading and making changes until my husband Aaron told me it was perfect. I hoped he was right. Portland deserved this day to be perfect.

CHAPTER 1

Brynne

March

"Mommy, mommy!" My eyes left the chicken that was cooking on the stove and I reached down to scoop up my daughter, Emmy Jo.

"What is it, sweetie?" I asked, reaching down to kiss her soft brown wisps of fine hair.

"I love you." She nuzzled her head into my neck and my heart melted. She had that effect on me at least a hundred times a day since she was born nearly four years ago. My daughter was my life, my world, my greatest joy. And she loved me.

"I love you too, baby. So much." I squeezed her tighter and closed my eyes, enjoying the moment of holding my baby girl. If only we could give her a sibling. Stop, I told myself firmly. No reason to start getting upset. Tonight Aaron and I were hosting dinner for my best friend Portland and her husband Trent, and I didn't need to be agonizing why I wasn't pregnant yet after almost a year of trying.

"I love you too, my gorgeous ladies." My husband walked in at that moment and joined our group, kissing Emmy Jo on the head and then my lips. "Hi, babe."

"Hey, hon. How was work?"

"Just fine. Think we'll have a new job coming our way shortly when the strip by Grand Avenue starts getting sold. Should make for a busy summer."

"That's great news! Will you need to hire more on for that?"

"Depends on how fast stores need to be up and how many we can get at once."

"You know if you ever need me to come back..."

"I know, Brynne. Thank you, but I don't think we will. I told you we would be fine. Not that I don't miss seeing my beautiful wife in the office every day." He winked and gave me another kiss. "EJ, what do you say we give Mommy some time to finish dinner. You and me, living room, toys, stat!" Emmy Jo squirmed out of my arms and took off racing towards the living room. "We'll stay out of your hair, but if you need help just holler." And my husband was off, leaving me back in the kitchen by myself.

I smiled as I gave the chicken my attention once again. I knew I had a lot to be grateful for, my daughter and my husband topping that list. Before Emmy Jo was born, I worked as a secretary/accountant/ office manager for my husband's growing construction and interior design business. Aaron had a knack for being able to design plans in his head, not only for a store's exterior construction, but for the interior as well. He started working construction with his dad back in grade school, and took over and expanded the family business after college. His dad retired early because of Aaron's progress, and he rewarded our little family every year with a getaway, always to the most beautiful places. Last year it was the Dominican Republic, this year will be St. Lucia. Aaron and I are thinking of going just the two of this year, as another honeymoon-type trip. More like a baby-making trip.

I frowned, turning the heat down on the chicken and stirring the penne noodles on the other burner. I had to stop worrying about our chances to conceive. We made Emmy Jo without even trying.

She was a classic honeymoon baby, born ten months after we were married. We honeymooned in Hawaii, a joint wedding present from our families so we could spend a blissful eleven days together on the island, enjoying the surf and sand and romantic sunsets. We were only twenty-one, so a few months after our return when I started throwing up seemingly every hour on the hour, pregnancy never even entered our thoughts. It was only after Portland convinced me to take a test that we saw our romantic trip had left us knocked up.

But we weren't scared or angry – quite the opposite. We were thrilled to be starting a family, and couldn't wait to meet Baby Ropert (we decided to stay surprised on the gender, so we just called her by our last name until she was born). Sure, it was a little sooner than our original plans to wait at least three years after marriage, but what's meant to be is meant to be. Aaron started baby-proofing the house as soon as he heard the news (after smooching me and rubbing my belly) and making design plans for the nursery. Our parents were over the moon to welcome their first grandchild on each side, probably even more so because Aaron and I were both only children. Emmy Jo was such a blessing for the whole family.

I drained the noodles and kept them in the strainer, passing it to the sink to wait. I quickly added a few ingredients – butter and flour – mixing them together in the previous pasta pot and turning the heat on again. I measured out two cups of milk and whisked that into the pot, watching with satisfaction as the sauce began to thicken up. I added in some dry ranch mix and shredded cheese, then dumped in the chicken and noodles, mixing together our dinner.

About four months into my pregnancy, Aaron thought it would be best if I gave up my job and took it easy. While I enjoyed working with my husband and couldn't complain about the position, I knew it wasn't what I was destined for. But I understood that I was lucky. Aaron and I met as college freshmen at the University of Southern

Maine, but Aaron didn't graduate and I only managed to get my associates degree in Business Administration with an accounting emphasis. Aaron's dad was constantly asking for his help with the business and just after midterms during our first year, Aaron realized he was better off at home with the family, making his transition to business owner.

I kept the chicken pasta in the pot to keep it warm, and went to the fridge to find and finish preparing dessert. I pulled out the bowl containing the strawberry cheesecake salad Emmy Jo and I started making this afternoon, and dug out the marshmallows from a drawer and grabbed a few bananas from the hanging rack. I pulled back the lid and the scent of cheesecake and strawberries wafted up, and I smiled in memory of Emmy Jo sticking her nose in the whipped topping to get a whiff and coming up with it all over her face. Hopefully nobody minded she had gotten a head start.

Even though Aaron and I had only been dating for a year, I was devastated when he told me he was moving back to Delany, Maine to help his father. Aaron seemed just as crushed as I was, and often talked about me moving back with him. Our short year together had quickly made Aaron not just my boyfriend, but my best friend. We did everything together, we would stay up late in the night talking, we understood each other. He let me be me, and I never felt I had to change or be anything other than myself around him. I was a little worried we were too young for such a big commitment, though. We were nineteen, far too young to have found the person we would settle down with. But I knew Aaron was special. He was caring, considerate, thoughtful...and he gave me that *feeling*. That feeling that let me imagine walking down the aisle towards him, that feeling of being loved forever, that feeling of...love.

I sliced up the strawberries, not able to resist slipping one into my mouth. I swiftly cut up the bananas and added those and the strawberries to the mix, whipping everything around with a soft spatula to coat the added fruit. I put the bowl back in the fridge where it would wait until after dinner, and went back to the chicken pasta. After ensuring it was still warm but not getting hot and dry, I grabbed four plates and Emmy Jo's favorite Princess Belle dish from the cabinet and started setting the table.

After the first year of college ended and talking about every single detail the move would entail, I accepted Aaron's offer to move to his hometown of Delany. I finished out my courses over the next year online to get my degree while Aaron worked full-time. My parents were fairly shocked when I told them my plans. They had met Aaron occasionally while we were at USM and I brought him home with me plenty of times, but I didn't think they understood the extent and seriousness of our relationship. But my parents had always firmly believed in me and supported me, and this step was no different. Both my mom and dad helped me pack up my room and belongings from my childhood home in Sweeny, only a twenty minute drive from Delany. I never thought taking the step to leave home to attend college would result in taking the step of moving in with my boyfriend of one year. But I'd never looked back or doubted my decision. Aaron jokes that the only reason he went to college was to find his wife – and he did.

I was just putting the last fork in place when Aaron and Emmy Jo came tearing into the kitchen, both with red faces. "Mommy, mommy! I'm hungry!" Emmy Jo shrieked, running to me and reaching up. I stooped down to grab her, hauling her to my hip.

"We just have to wait for Aunt Portland and Uncle Trent to get here, sweetie. Then we can eat, eat, eat!" I pretended to munch on her fingers and she squealed in delight.

"What time were they expected? It's getting kind of late for them," Aaron noted, glancing at the kitchen clock which read 6:21.

"She said around six, so they should be here anytime hopefully. I don't want the chicken getting dry."

"I'm sure it will taste fabulous no matter what."

I smiled at my husband as he reached into the fridge for a soda. After making the decision (conceding to Aaron) that I would stop working while pregnant, I went a bit stir-crazy and my mind went into overdrive. The outcome was a new business under our belts. I opened EJ Reads, my own little bookstore and café, ten months after Emmy Jo was born. It wasn't a big income maker for the family, but it was mine and I loved it. Aaron's mom helped around the store and I only had two other people on the payroll, but it did well enough and we had just found ourselves in the black for the first time. Aaron was not amused at first when I showed him my ideas, saying that when he suggested I take a break from his business he meant a break from working, period. It took some convincing and even some begging, but after a while he came around – especially once his mom volunteered to help out anytime.

The doorbell rang then and moments later Portland swept into the room, her husband Trent following behind her. "Hello, my darling! Clams?" She thrust a take-out container from Charlie's down the road into my hands and pecked me on the cheek. "I had to stop and grab something because this day was simply crazy. No time in the kitchen for me!"

I laughed, setting the clams on the counter. "No worries, Port, Charlie's is always delicious. Thanks for bringing them."

"And some wine for the lady." Trent handed over two bottles of red, while Portland opened the drawer for the wine opener. "I got these from a client and they're supposed to be bad ass."

"Trent! Children!" Portland hissed, cutting her eyes to Emmy Jo who was hugging her knees. She scooped down and picked her up, hugging my daughter to her cheek. "Don't listen to your Uncle Trent. He's just a goofball. How are you, sweet EJ?"

"Good! I got to wear pajamas to school today!" Emmy Jo's eyes lit up as she told Portland all about wearing her Disney Princess pajamas/dress to daycare that day. Emmy Jo loved to call it "school" because she said grown-ups went to school, and she was practically a grown-up herself. I didn't even want to speculate on what her teenage years would bring.

I took out wine glasses and opened one bottle, letting it breathe before pouring the real grown-ups each a glass. I refilled Emmy Jo's sippy cup with milk and got her plate together first. "Okay, EJ, let's get you to the table."

I got her settled in with some pasta, a few strawberries and bananas leftover from making the dessert, and a cracker bar that had Spongebob Square Pants on it. Tucking a napkin in her lap, I kissed the top of her head before heading back to the center island. I loved that our kitchen was an open concept and easily big enough to fit many people, which came in handy when we hosted holidays or other parties at our home. The kitchen table fit ahead in front of of the back porch door, and we got a great view of the beautiful landscape that filled Delany. The sunsets were my particular favorite; I loved nothing more than sitting on the porch with Aaron and Emmy Jo to watch them at night.

The four of us filled our plates and sat at the table, Portland next to me and our husbands across from us. It was a Thursday night tradition to have our friends over, and even though Portland and I saw each other nearly every day, we never ran out of things to talk about.

"How was the store today?" I asked her, taking a bite from the pasta and savoring the taste on my tongue. I was already planning the menu for next week in my head.

"I think everyone is eager for the warmer days to be here, because I'm noticing an increase in the colder drinks over the warm ones,"

Portland said, taking a sip of wine. "We'll have to think about getting a larger supply for drinks like lemonade, iced teas, and that sort of thing with the next order."

"Okay, good to know. I'll be sure to jot that down. I'll be putting in an order probably in two weeks again, so that should be pretty good timing."

"Mommy, can we go to the beach again this year?" Emmy Jo asked, her eyes wide with excitement at the prospect of seeing the ocean.

"Yes, of course, honey. I'm sure we'll practically live there this year now that you're a little older."

"Dad, I'm going to live at the beach!" Emmy Jo shrieked in Aaron's face as he reached over to grab the napkin off the floor and place it back in her lap. "All the kids at school will be so jealous of me!"

"You are one lucky crab, that's for sure." Aaron tweaked her ear and shot a wink at me. I grinned back, but still felt a little deflated on the inside. How in the world was it that we were not pregnant yet?

"Everything okay, B?" Portland asked, peering at me.

"Oh, just fine. Just thinking about the store again is all." I flashed her a grin, and we continued to talk about EJ Reads. Portland was one of the two on the payroll (the other being a high school junior, Serena) and she seemed to enjoy her job. Portland didn't actually need to work thanks to Trent's high-paying career, but she wanted a purpose, a reason not to stay in her pajamas all day, so when I opened the store it seemed natural for her to come on. She helped man the checkout counter, the cafe, stocking the shelves, noting what to order, and keeping the place neat and tidy. She was such an asset to the store, and I was glad she enjoyed it. Trent worked for a fitness company which he invested in years back, and he was always on the road selling vitamins and supplements and workout equipment to gyms in the area. He was gone a lot so I knew Portland liked having an outlet such as the store to focus on, but the money he made was really great. Who knew gyms could be so profitable?

The dinner flowed along as it usually did, the men talking sports and how baseball was just around the corner and which games they would want to attend at Fenway. They reflected back on the Superbowl that was a few weeks ago, and still grumbled about the New England Patriots losing to the Green Bay Packers. Portland and I chatted some more about EJ Reads, Trent's upcoming travel schedule, and the 5K Cancer walk/run we had signed up for that would take place the last Sunday in March.

"Lisa has the T-shirts made and I'll pick them up next week for us," Portland said, shoveling the last bite of pasta in her mouth. "Mmm, this is delicious, Brynne. I still don't see how you and Aaron aren't overweight slobs."

"I wish I had time to cook like this more often. Aaron has a big new job prospect coming up and then with the store and Emmy Jo...the time just isn't there anymore." I sighed, pushing back my chair and grabbing my empty plate. Portland stood and followed me as well, leaving the guys at the table to continue discussing who would have more home runs this year and something about a green monster. I could never keep track of the sports, games, and athletes they droned on about.

"What job is that for Aaron?" Portland asked, opening the dishwasher and starting to load it.

"That strip on Grand is apparently starting to sell space, so he's going to put a bid on it soon. It would be great to secure even a handful of the stores that come in, if not all."

Portland nodded, her shiny blonde hair catching some of the last rays from the kitchen window. "Sounds like that could be a money-maker if it went through."

"Sure could. It would be nice to take some pressure off from opening the store."

"I thought the books just went to black?"

"They did, but that was literally just two months ago, and now we have to strive to keep sales up and costs down. The first year was a little tough and we had to scale back in some areas, so I know Aaron will be glad if he can get a few more jobs on the schedule."

Portland nodded and then walked back to Aaron and Trent, grabbing both their empty plates. She didn't say anything as she continued to load the dishwasher, nor made a sound when I opened the dessert bowl.

"I made strawberry cheesecake salad, Port. Does it smell good?" I teasingly drew circles under her nose with the bowl, but she just smiled back at me weakly. "Is everything okay?" Her sudden mood change startled me.

"Oh, yes, everything's fine. This smells delicious. I'm going to run to the restroom quick before I dig in." She turned abruptly on her heel and walked out of the room. I heard the bathroom door down the hallway click shut, and then water running. I shook my head, making a mental note to check in with my friend when it was just the two of us, then turned back to the kitchen table. "Who wants dessert?"

CHAPTER 2

Portland

I shut the door behind me and took a deep breath. Turning the faucet on, I gave my face gentle pats with the cold water, so I didn't ruin my makeup but was still able to calm down. It was ridiculous that I was getting so upset. Brynne didn't do anything wrong, she was just being Brynne. But her comment about scaling back and the fight I'd had with Trent on the way over made my stomach upset. I just needed a minute for myself, to breathe and be able to stop smiling through the pain.

I glanced at myself in the mirror, hoping no one else could see the bags under my eyes from the lack of sleep the night before. I had visited my hair stylist just yesterday so my blonde tresses were smooth and shiny, but that was about the only glowing quality I had at the time. I itched to be able to say something to my friend, but I sensed Brynne was going through something herself at the moment, and didn't want to burden her with my (probably silly) problems. Knowing Brynne, she would drop everything and focus on me and only me until we worked through it. She might even have me take some time off from the store, and I really didn't want that. EJs was my escape.

Realizing I had been in the bathroom long enough, I patted my face and hands dry on the lavender towel that was hanging next to the sink, to match the lavender hand soap and lavender diffuser Brynne had set up. That made me smile, to think about my friend who loved nothing more than her house being in order.

"There she is! Portland, I put some cheesecake salad on a plate for you. I hope you like it." Brynne handed me a small plate that was filled with the delicious smelling dessert, and I smiled at her gratefully.

"And I helped make it!" Emmy Jo squealed, before digging back into her own piece.

I sat in my regular seat next to Brynne, across from my husband. "You did an excellent job, missy. And, mmm, it's so delicious!" I said that last bit around a bite, and wasn't lying. Brynne was a natural in the kitchen.

"It's about time for you to start thinking about bed, don't you think?" Brynne directed her question at Emmy Jo.

"No! I get to stay up with the grown-ups tonight." Emmy Jo pouted and folded her arms. One little finger poked out and grabbed a strawberry, quickly stuffing it in her mouth before folding her arms again like nothing had happened. I took a sip of wine to hide my smile.

"Grown-ups also have to go to school in the morning, and you don't want to fall asleep next to Guy, do you?" Brynne continued, looking in mock horror at her daughter.

EJ's eyes grew wide as she considered this. "He might put glue in my hair, or color marker on my face, momma. I don't want to fall asleep next to him!"

"Well, then, let's get you to bed on time so you don't have to worry about that."

Emmy Jo took one more large bite of her dessert and raced out of the room. Brynne sat for a moment watching her retreating form, then laughed. "I didn't think that would work that well. She's been complaining about this Guy for a few weeks since the seating arrangements changed at daycare, but I really think she might have a crush on him. I'll be back."

"Glue in hair and markers on the face? I thought that only happened at parties where you were the first to pass out," I said.

Aaron stood from the table. "I'm going to go say good-night. Let's hope those wild parties stay away from Emmy Jo for a long, long time." He winked at me before leaving. I shook my head. Aaron was one of the most over-protective fathers I had ever met, but it was cute. He was a great dad and a great husband, and I knew how lucky both Brynne and Emmy Jo were.

"Well, it's just you and me, babe. How about a quickie on the porch?" Trent leered at me, and I glared back.

"You know as well as I do that it takes Emmy Jo about five minutes to get settled. They'll be back in no time."

"I said quickie. I can wrap it up in two minutes tops."

"Wow, that is so romantic and really turns me on, Trent. Please, keep talking."

"I was just trying to liven things up around here. Sue me for finding my wife attractive."

I rolled my eyes. "Oh, don't be such a baby. We had sex two days ago before you left, so don't act like you're all deprived either."

"What is wrong with you tonight? You've been acting weird all day."

The hair on my arms rose. Trent had been able to see through me too? Brynne was an obvious one, she was my best friend, but Trent didn't usually notice – or care – if my moods were off. Shit.

"I'm just not feeling the best today. I hope I'm not coming down with a cold or anything. The weather shifts are starting to get to me I think."

Trent peered into my face for a moment, making me want to

shake under his stare. "You do look a little pale. Did you sleep well last night?"

I shook my head. "Not really. That's probably a part of it too."

"Do you want to leave soon so you can try to tuck in early? I can probably round up a sleeping pill or two for you to take."

And he's flipped to the caring, compassionate husband. I just never knew who I was going to get from one moment to the next anymore. "No, that's okay. I need to talk with Brynne about the store some more. I'm sure I'll be okay."

Brynne and Aaron re-entered the kitchen. "She's down for the count. I swear the second her head hit the pillow she was asleep," Brynne said, grabbing her glass of wine from the island. "I have the latest *Housewives* show DVR'd for us. Take our party to the living room?" Brynne queried, looking at me.

"You got it." I stood and grabbed my wine glass, following her into the living room where she powered up their 60-inch flat-screen TV. We loved watching the *Housewives* shows and dissecting all the reality TV drama.

"And we should probably get in a game of pool or two," Aaron said, clapping Trent on the back.

My husband stood. "I'll grab the beers and hit the john while you get the table ready. Winner from last week breaks. Oh, yes – that's me."

Aaron just shook his head as he walked towards their staircase. "Lucky shot on the eight, lucky shot on the eight."

The men disappeared into the depths of the basement, or the half man-cave as it was also called. It was so large that Aaron didn't actually need the whole thing, so half the space was his game room: another big-screen TV, a couple of recliners, a full fridge that was always stocked, a bar, a pool table, two dart boards, a foosball table, and an old-time jukebox covered his space. The other half was used for storage, a full guest bedroom complete with a private bath, and a second office that was used to keep old records of construction jobs. Even though the house Trent and I had designed and built from the ground-up to all of the specifications we desired once we were married, it would never compare to the spacious Ropert abode.

Brynne and I became engrossed in the show, watching the women fight (literally!), moan, complain, get dressed up, party their faces off, then fight (literally!), moan and complain some more about how terrible their lives were. Sometimes I wondered how I could possibly enjoy a show like this, but something about it just reeled me in.

"What days are you at the store next week?" Brynne asked after the first episode was finished.

"Every day but Wednesday. Trent is in Canpart most of the week."

She nodded. "That's great. I'm going to volunteer probably on Tuesday then for Emmy Jo's class. They keep calling for more and more mothers to volunteer during special events at the school, and I really want to participate a few times."

"What's the event on Tuesday?"

"Field trip to the aquarium. Not only would I like to go myself, but I would love to see Emmy Jo's face when she takes it all in. She's just a water-lover, pure and through."

"When do swimming lessons start? You'll sign her up, right?"

"Of course. I think you can do it as young as two, but there was no way I was doing that. Three is even a stretch. Next year for sure I'll get her signed up, and hopefully be a little more comfortable with the idea of a stranger holding my kid in the pool."

"I'm sure it will be okay. I bet they wear the floatie things for a long time in those classes."

"I know, I know. I'm sure it's safe and all, but what if she sticks her head in the water for the fun of it and then drowns? It just freaks me out to think about it."

I patted my friends arm, shooting her a smile. She didn't always seem like an over-protective mom, but that side could definitely show from time to time.

Brynne and I continued to watch our shows, and it was near eleven when the guys came back up and Trent and I headed home. I hugged Aaron and Brynne, thanking them for their hospitality and the food, and Trent grabbed my hand as we headed for the car.

"That was a fun night. I beat Aaron two out of three," Trent bragged, opening the car door for me. It was never a good night for Trent unless he beat somebody at something – such a charming trait in the man I married.

"Good for you," I said, as he slid in and started the engine.

He glanced over at me. "Seriously, everything okay? You've seemed off the whole night."

Well, at least I knew I would never get the urge to be an actor. I wasn't fooling anybody apparently. "I really just think I'm coming down with something. Let's just get home so I can crawl into bed. I don't even have to be up early tomorrow, B is going to open the store. I can sleep in a little."

"That sounds good. Maybe you're working too hard at that store. You know you don't need to anyway." His chest puffed out a bit in pride as he said this. I knew he wanted to bring home the bacon and be the sole supporter, but I was not wired to be a housewife.

"It's okay. It's not like I work forty hours a week or anything. And it keeps me busy when you're gone."

Trent reached over and settled his hand on my knee. "I have some bad news on that front."

"Oh?"

"I might have to be gone longer than usual next week. Some

clients in Marsan want me to swing back and check out some equipment they're having issues with and drop off more supplements. I guess they're selling them like hotcakes."

"How long do you think you'll be gone?" My pulse started to quicken. If he was gone that meant I could get back in his office, poke around one more time...

"Probably an added week. Marsan is about four hours north of Canpart so I'll try to hit up the other gyms and locations around there since I won't want to do that drive again anytime soon."

I nodded my head, trying to look contrite. "Well, okay. I'll miss you. Maybe I'll just pick up some extra time at the store. I get so bored in the house by myself."

"Maybe we'll have to start trying to fix that problem."

I looked at Trent, who wiggled his eyebrows suggestively. "A baby?"

"Yeah, why not? You like kids, Emmy Jo is a riot. We have the house and the money. It could help entertain you while I'm gone."

I wasn't sure having a kid purely for entertainment purposes was the right reason to get pregnant. And how I could have a child with him when I might have just uncovered...something. "Maybe." I tried to sound indifferent. "They also seem like a lot of work and Brynne is always stressing about one thing or another when it comes to EJ and her health or safety or schooling." Kind of. She seemed pretty relaxed to me, but I'm sure all moms went through stress.

"Well, let's just think about it some more then. Or just practice for the time being."

My stomach flipped, but I still flashed a smile.

ßⱷ

I lay in bed by myself that night, as Trent said he still had some reports to look at. I flipped onto my stomach, my favorite sleeping position, and tried to will myself to sleep. My mind wouldn't shut off. I flashed to the papers I found in Trent's desk last night, purely on accident. I had never thought to snoop on my husband of two years. I was trying to find our tax returns from last year to give to the accountant, as we were severely behind and the April deadline was just around the corner. I had tried calling Trent to see where they were, but his phone was going straight to voicemail. I knew he was driving home and sometimes his service cut in and out, so I didn't think anything of it. I decided to find the papers myself, mostly out of boredom and the need to do something.

Trent's office in our 2200 square foot ranch home was on the first floor, all the way to the east. I rarely ventured in there as I had no reason to, only popping in when Trent was working. It felt a little foreign being there, but I sat at his desk chair and looked around me. His desk wasn't just some shoddy little thing tucked into the corner, no, the desk ran almost the full length of the wall, big enough for three people to easily fit at. He had one desktop computer set up and a laptop as well, and he carried yet another laptop with him on business trips. A printer that doubled as a scanner sat on one corner, and a fax machine on another. He had multiple calendars hung up with agendas scribbled on the majority of the dates, and another smaller calendar that sat to the right of the desktop. It was opened to that date, March 14, and scribbled on there was "Petosi." He had been in that town for the past two nights, and was due home late in the night.

After some searching, I finally found the drawer that seemed to hold important records. Our passports were in there, our wedding license, birth certificates, and deed to the house. I found the titles to both our vehicles, but no tax information. I frowned, trying to think of another spot he would have them. I slipped all the papers back in the appropriate files and shut the drawer and when I did, a single piece of paper had floated down to me from somewhere at the top of the desk. I grabbed the sheet and read over the words, my eyes growing wide, then squinting as I read and re-read. My body turned cold as I sat in shock, trying to process what I had read. When I realized I'd been sitting there for probably thirty minutes doing absolutely nothing I jumped, understanding that Trent could walk through the door at any minute and find me. Then what would I say?

Carefully, I pushed myself up and climbed onto the office chair, putting the piece of paper back where I thought it had come from. From my new vantage point, I saw the top of his desk was riddled with other papers and...a calendar. I swallowed hard as I peered closer and saw what was written in under March 13. My stomach heaving, I quickly left the office after righting the chair to its original spot, and fled to the bathroom.

I blinked back tears in bed as I forced myself to calm my mind. Trent had some explaining to do sure, but how did I tell him what I had found? Did that really even matter in the grand scheme of things? But knowing the Trent as of lately, he would try to turn this around on me and make me look like the bad person. I squeezed my eyes shut and prayed for sleep. I just wanted to sleep, to forget about what I had found. The day had been torturous enough, trying to make everything seem like it was hunky dory and nothing out of place. And what would tomorrow bring? More questions. And next week – Trent would be gone for two weeks. Would he be going where he said he was? What was he actually doing on his trips away?

The bedroom door opened and I saw Trent enter the room, already in just his boxers. I let my breathing become even so he would think I was asleep.

He plugged his cell phone in and set it on the nightstand, then pulled the covers back and crawled in. I felt his cold feet touch mine and jerked involuntarily. "Are you awake?" he whispered. I could feel his erection pressing into my back, and knew what he wanted. He probably touched me on purpose.

"Mmmph," I mumbled, not opening my eyes.

"Port. You awake?" he asked again, clearly not getting the hint as his hand wandered to my breast.

I rolled away and made more sleeping noises, begging in my mind for him to leave me alone. He stayed quiet for another moment, then finally rolled the other way.

I was off the hook – at least for one night.

CHAPTER 3

Brynne

I closed the curtains in the living room, watching Trent lovingly tuck Portland into their vehicle. Aaron came up behind me and encircled his arms around my waist. "Whatcha thinking about, love?" he asked, his breath tickling my ear.

"Just how happy I am for Portland. She really deserves a man like Trent, someone to finally take care of her and treat her right."

"I agree. I'm glad we can have them over so often. Trent's a nice guy. We were throwing around some travel ideas too for the spring."

"I'm glad you think so. What ideas do you boys have this year?"

"The typical ones of course – Fenway Park for a few games, and we discussed heading up to New York to catch a game at Yankee stadium. You ladies can come too of course and shop your little hearts out."

I turned to Aaron, a broad smile finding my face. "Really? It's been too long since we got away to New York. Portland will be ecstatic."

"I thought you might like that idea. Just a couple's trip; we'll ask my parents to watch over Emmy Jo. Or your parents if they want to come up and even housesit for us."

"I can't wait! I'll call Portland so we can start making our travel arrangements! When is the game? What month? Which hotel should we stay at?" I was already getting too far ahead of myself, but I was crazy excited. Aaron and I last visited New York when I was four months pregnant and while we still enjoyed ourselves immensely, I was tired and my feet ached the whole time. It would be nice to go again not with child – unless something happened, of course. I wouldn't complain this time around.

Aaron must have read my thoughts because he kissed me deeply then, twirling a finger in my hair. "Let's move this to the bedroom, shall we, Mrs. Ropert?"

I giggled like a little girl, always my reaction when my husband called me by my married name. Luckily it only happened when he said it, or else I would be pretty embarrassed after four years of marriage. My stomach burned with desire for him, and I took his hand and blew out the candles we had lit in the living room. "I'll lead the way."

After making love, I rested my head on Aaron's chest and felt it rise and fall with his deep breaths. I shut my eyes and said a silent prayer like I did every night: giving thanks for life, for my husband, my gorgeous daughter, and my friends. I was a lucky one.

ജ‌ഝ

The next morning I was up at 5:30, ready to get a start on the day. My morning schedule was as followed: complete a Yoga DVD in the living room, shower, get dressed, rise Emmy Jo, get her ready for daycare, wake up Aaron so he would get in the shower, make breakfast of scrambled eggs, bacon and toast, feed my family, pack up my work bag and Emmy Jo's daycare bag, pile everything including my daughter into the car, and kiss Aaron good-bye before backing out of the garage.

I pointed my Hyundai Tucson (with top safety ratings and an

awesome panoramic sunroof, also in a sharp pearl color) towards the daycare and was off, with Emmy Jo dozing in her car seat. Her daycare was only a six minute drive from our house, and on days I didn't have to be at the bookstore (and when the weather was a bit warmer) I often just walked her up and jogged back home. I pulled into the busy parking lot and up to the drop off station, waving at fellow parents and children along the way. I navigated the SUV to the side and put it into park, hopping out to get Emmy Jo, who had somehow managed to wake up on our short drive. Her green eyes that matched my own looked back at me, and she easily helped me unbuckle her so she could climb out.

Miss Amanda's helper came over to grab Emmy Jo, a young woman named Amber. "Hello, Emmy Jo! Happy Friday, Mrs. Ropert," she said, a wide smile on her face.

"Good morning, Amber. I hate to dash so fast but I'm at the store today," I said, handing over EJ's bag to her.

"No worries at all! Let's get you right in, Emmy Jo. Do you remember what we're doing today?" Amber asked, crouching so she was at eye level with EJ.

"Um – finger painting!" Emmy Jo answered proudly, looking at me with wide eyes. "Mommy, did you remember to pack a big shirt for me?"

I smiled at her. "I sure did, sweetie. It's in your bag for you. I hope you have a good time. Daddy will pick you up today, okay?"

"Okay! What should I paint for you?"

My heart melted, such a common occurrence Emmy Jo brought on. "Surprise me. I know I'll love whatever you decide on. Now give Mommy a kiss!"

Emmy Jo obediently put her arms up and I swooped her up on my hip, giving her a kiss and a tight squeeze before setting her down. "You be good for Amber and Miss Amanda today. Have fun, girls!"

Emmy Jo and Amber waved before they set off into the building. I waited until they were out of sight before driving off, this time to Starbucks for a quick mocha and then to the bookstore.

I unlocked the main doors to EJ Reads and set off for the office, where I deposited my purse, work bag, and coffee on the desk. I didn't bother locking the main doors behind me, even though we didn't open for another forty minutes or so at nine o'clock. If someone wandered in great, but those chances were fairly slim. The bookstore never got real busy in the morning; sometimes the odd customer would wander in for a coffee, but most workers were already in the office by the time we opened. I answered a few emails and then went out to the cash register to get it opened for the day. I counted the cash that was in there – sixty dollars, mostly in small bills, and set to work turning on the lights. Everything looked clean and in order from the night before, which I knew was thanks to Portland and her meticulous closing routine. She didn't leave anything undusted, a book out of place, or a cup on the counter when she closed down.

I went into the small café area next, to turn on the machines and get some of the pastries out. The café was mostly for drinks – coffee and smoothies were always a hit, but I liked to have some pastries and sandwiches available as well. We had a small oven in the kitchen that I used, though I would much rather do the baking at home, but code regulations state any cooking/baking needed to be done on business grounds.

After filling the pastry jar and making a pot of coffee, I went back to the front area near the cash register. I had brought along the scrapbook project I was recently working on, filled with pictures from last year. I had photos of our trip to the Dominican Republic, Emmy Jo's third birthday party, a few from the new stores that Aaron designed, and plenty of random get together's to fill the pages. I loved scrapbooking, and made a special book for big events such as our wedding and Emmy Jo's birth, but I loved putting together one for each year so it would be easy to look back at all the memories that were made. Working on it at the store helped me get some quiet time and reflect back on everything that happened. I giggled when I saw a photo of Emmy Jo with pink frosting smeared on her face from her birthday cake, and smiled at a photo of myself and Portland having a spa day during our girls' weekend last summer when we traveled to New Hampshire just the two of us.

At just after ten the first customer walked in, heading right to the café. "Hello, Mr. Jones. What can I get for you?"

"Hello, Brynne. How are you this morning?" Mr. Jones worked as a loan specialist at the bank right across from the store. He visited darn near every day, and was one of my favorite customers.

"Doing well, doing well. Any big plans for the weekend?" I popped in behind the café doors and poured him a cup of coffee, securing a lid on and passing it over to him. I knew he was coming for a coffee, and awaited any further order he might have.

"Nothing too exciting. Anna and I might take the girls to that Disney movie hitting theaters. How about you? And can I grab that jelly pastry right here? Didn't bring a big lunch so I thought I could fit in a dessert today." He winked at me.

I packaged up the pastry and slid that across to him as well. "And it's Friday – always a day to eat dessert! We don't have anything planned out either. Just a good weekend to relax at home for us I think."

We walked over to the cash register and I rang him up, making more small talk about the weather changes and the weekend and how Mrs. Jones was doing. Mr. Jones had two young daughters with his wife, Cara and Lara, and a boy on the way. Luckily, she was due before the summer would really heat up.

Around lunchtime I packed away the scrapbooking items as I

knew the store would pick up. The café kept up a steady stream of drink and sandwich orders, and a customer even purchased a book. As such an avid reader it made me sad to think that EJ Reads wouldn't survive if it was solely a bookstore. With the digital age and eReaders out there, book stores just weren't in high demand anymore. Aaron suggested once I even start selling items such as Kindles and Nooks, but I didn't have the faintest idea how to accomplish that nor did I really want to. A physical book to touch, open, and smell was what made me happy.

As I was getting wrapped up in the thought of books, the door opened once again and Portland stepped through. She headed towards the front desk, stopping to straighten a few books on her way and chat with a customer perusing the shelves. "Hey, B. How's the day going?"

"Fairly steady. How was your morning?" I noted that Portland looked a little pale, which was unusual for her. Her skin always seemed to be a tan, even in the months the sun refused to shine. I wondered if she might be getting sick.

"Oh, okay. I slept in which was amazing. Really needed that."

"You feeling okay?" I watched her closely as she stuck her purse under the counter and then straightened, smoothing down her pale blue button-up shirt.

"Yeah, I'm okay. I thought maybe I might be coming down with something, but I think I was just tired. The sleep really helped."

I regarded her closely for another moment. Her smile didn't seem to meet her eyes, but if she wasn't ready to talk about what was bothering her, I wouldn't press it. Portland always came around in time.

We became friends in college after we were paired up to room together. I couldn't help but feel intimidated the first time I saw her in the dorm – satin blonde hair almost to her waist, pale blue eyes, tanned skin, long legs...I definitely didn't think she would be as friendly as she was, nor did I think she would take a liking to me. I was about four inches shorter than Portland, with boring brown hair that I wore past my shoulders in college but cut into a short bob after having Emmy Jo. My green eyes were my best feature, as I didn't have long legs or big boobs or anything that Portland could showcase. I looked like the meek Mary Anne from The Baby-Sitters Club and Portland was definitely the fashionable Stacey.

I didn't expect to hit it off with her right from the start, but we became fast friends. Whether we were in the library studying, at parties drinking underage, or taking trips to the beach on the weekends, we did everything together after meeting. I cried when I told Portland my decision to follow Aaron back to Delany, and was bowled over when she announced she wanted to come with me. Portland was an only child and just had her dad after her mom passed away, so she didn't have much tying her to her hometown of Springfield, and hadn't made plans on moving back there after college. I was immensely happy she decided to move to Delany, and we had a blast searching for an apartment to get her set up in. Sometimes I thought our friendship could be a bit strained, because it was like we never figured out how to be grown-ups with each other, to talk about problems and issues that really mattered. I think Portland held a lot back from me because she assumed I couldn't relate to the hardships she had been through, but she was wrong. I wished I could figure out how to fix that issue between us, but usually our friendship was so strong that I didn't worry about it.

"Have you eaten lunch?" I asked her then, feeling my stomach rumble.

"Yeah, I ate at home. Sorry."

"That's okay, I was just going to grab a sandwich from the café. I think the lunch crowd has probably settled enough that I can sneak a sandwich and not have to worry." I walked over to the cafe and plucked a turkey, cheese, and avocado sandwich from the bunch, along with a bottle of water from the fridge. Heading back to the desk I took my seat next to Portland, who had pulled up the internet on the computer.

I opened the plastic container and took a bite, loving the crunch the avocado provided. "Hey, I almost forgot. Did Trent mention anything about New York to you last night?"

Portland looked at me with scrunched brows. "New York? No."

"Aaron said him and Trent are talking about going there for a Sox/Yankees game, which means we get to hit the shops! He wasn't sure exactly of the schedule yet, but I'm ready to start planning! It's been too long since I've been there."

"That does sound like fun. I could definitely use a vacation."

I peered at Portland again, taking another bite of my sandwich. Something was off about her, but I couldn't put my finger on what. "Same here. I'll start putting a list together of things we have to see, stores not to miss, and some of the great restaurants we can try. Hopefully we can get a three day weekend."

"What about the store?"

"I'm sure Aaron's mom would be happy to watch over it for us. And Serena would probably enjoy the extra spending money."

Portland nodded. "I'll start looking online too for things to do. Something to look forward to." She smiled and went back to the computer and I got back to my sandwich. We sat in silence for a while longer, until a customer walked in and headed for the café. Portland stood to help him, ringing Mr. Lewis up for two coffees.

I knew Portland's mood could shift a bit in the month of October, the month her mom died, but it was March now. I wondered briefly if everything was all right with Trent, but quickly dismissed that thought. Trent was such a perfect husband, and Portland really had a charmed life with him. They met when Trent was in town on business and it was love at first sight – honestly. Even though Trent lived a few towns north, he moved to Delany and they rented a home together right away, then bought land and started building their dream house after only four months of dating. I worried for a hot second that it was too soon, but it wasn't long before he put a ring on her finger and they were married in a beautiful ceremony by the water. I was her maid of honor and remember feeling such happiness for my friend, who looked like she stepped off the pages of a bridal magazine in her designer dress. Trent was older than her by three years, and he obviously knew what he wanted in life and didn't want to waste another second once he found Portland. I thought their love story was so romantic.

Portland and Trent could still act like they were in the honeymoon stage – lots of kisses, always holding hands, constantly texting when they were apart. If I could be honest, it sometimes could make me feel like Aaron and I weren't as in love as they were. I knew no relationship was the same and every couple was different, but when Portland would tell me about the romantic dates Trent would take her on and show me the lovey-dovey text messages she was sending him, it would make me feel just a tad bit insecure about my marriage. I tried my hardest not to compare us, but it just felt like she had such a perfect relationship and I'll admit it – I could get jealous. Not that I would ever get mad at Portland – who gets mad at their friend for being happy? And Portland really, really deserved all the happiness she got, after everything she went through with her mom.

"Trent told me last night he'll be gone for two weeks once he leaves on Monday," Portland said suddenly, breaking the silence.

I looked up from the scrapbooking I had started working on once again. "Two weeks? Eesh, that seems like a long time."

"Yeah, I guess he's hitting more cities than usual so he wants to get it all done in one swoop so he doesn't have to drive so far north again in a few weeks."

"That makes sense then. Maybe we should plan something for next weekend. I think I'm totally open."

"I think I would be up for just a girls' night – maybe do some of those mud masks and just watch movies at my house? It can get so lonely there when he's gone for so long."

"Let's plan on it. I'm always up for a good sleepover. A day to sleep in without Emmy Jo running around at six in the morning is like heaven." I smiled, thinking of how Emmy Jo was like a crazed child right after waking up – often then crashing just minutes later.

"Great. I think that is just what I need." Portland grinned at me, and I finally saw the smile in her eyes.

CHAPTER 4

Portland

I left the bookstore around 5:30 to grab a quick dinner before Brynne headed home for the night. I stopped by Charlie's even though I just had their clams the night before, but it was close, fast, and delicious. I stepped into the restaurant, immediately having the scent of seafood, fried food, and other diner smells seep into my nose – and my clothes. I stepped up to the counter and placed my order, just barely having time to tap out a text message to Trent before the food was ready.

I grabbed the bag and headed back out to the car, setting the food on the passenger seat before reading Trent's incoming text. He wanted to know if I would do a business dinner with him and a few of his associates tonight. After telling him I was eating Charlie's and had to close the store at eight, he asked if I would compromise and meet them out for drinks after.

I sighed, resting my head on the headrest and thinking before replying. I actually couldn't wait until he left on Monday, as I was itching to get back into his office and decide what the hell was going on with my husband – and possibly my marriage. Then I had to figure out where to go from there, if I would tell Brynne, what it meant for the rest of my life. I didn't think I could go much longer trying to pretend everything would be okay – and it had only been two days!

I pulled out of the parking lot before answering, because I knew if the car smelled like fried food tonight Trent would go postal. He loved the BMW 528i he bought last year but I didn't see the big deal about it – or what all those numbers meant. And I didn't understand Trent's love affair with the damn car – it seemed it was always in the shop needing some sort of work done. Knowing my husband, he just wanted to flash the car around to business associates and casually slip into conversations that he owned a BMW. I begged for a normal car – something like Brynne's trusty Tucson or even just a pickup trick, but Trent would hear none of that. When he had to travel he used the Lexus RX – that car was a bit better than the BMW, but still way too flashy in my mind.

I didn't come from much – well, anything – and I still didn't seem to fit into Trent's new lifestyle of throwing money around. My dad did his best to scrape by after Mom died, and I would always appreciate everything he did for me. He was a good man – the best – and Trent reminded me a lot of him when we first met. Not even just the appearance – blonde hair, blue eyes, over six feet and a solid build – but in their strength to succeed. Dad didn't want me to be embarrassed about having to wear Goodwill clothes or that he couldn't even afford a car after he had to pay back all the money Mom owed. He worked in construction and had a way with making beautiful items from wood – dressers, tables, you name it. Everything wood in our house had made been made from his hands. I had fond memories of hugging him once he was home, all sweaty and smelling like dirt or sawdust.

I looked like my dad with the blonde hair and blue eyes, and some people even joked that Trent and I looked like brother and sister. Speaking of Trent...I forced my thoughts away from Dad and typed out a message to him, agreeing to stop by The Window after I closed the store. I couldn't think of any excuse as to why I wouldn't

– I always accompanied Trent to any work event. I knew how much pride he had in his company and the growth he achieved over the years, and I used to love playing the proud wife.

"Hey, what'd you get?" Brynne called to me as I walked in. She was reading a book behind the counter, a cute pink book with a cupcake on it.

"Charlie's. I know it's terrible for me especially two nights in a row, but I only had the clams last night and I'm planning on going to the gym with you tomorrow. And I just had a craving for fried frog legs – don't laugh."

Brynne shrugged her shoulders, but I could see a smile creeping up. "No judging here. I like fried frog legs from time to time. Though I always craved them when I was pregnant...Oh my God! Are you pregnant?"

"What? No! Of course not! I would have told you the second I found out, B. Don't be silly."

"Sorry. Of course not. Of course you would tell me. Duh. It's just, well, you seem kinda off lately and then I was thinking about when I was pregnant and always making Aaron come home with the fried frog legs. Sorry. Sorry I said anything."

"Sorry, Brynne. If I've seemed...off." I wasn't sure I wanted to get into any details – or even if there were any details to give – and now was definitely not the right time. "Actually, Trent and I have been talking about possibly having a baby. But that's all, just talking," I rushed to say when I saw her eyes light up. "And it's been really recent, so I've just been thinking about it and having a baby and what changes that would bring. That's probably what you're noticing." I felt terrible lying to my best friend, especially since Trent casually dropped a line just the night before and probably wasn't even serious and I hadn't given it a second thought but...it would distract Brynne long enough for me to figure out what to do.

"Oh, Portland, still! That's so exciting to even be talking about it! You know I'm just dying over here for you to finally pop out a baby. Think of the play dates we can have, or me being able to chat with you about cracked nipples without you wanting to toss your cookies."

I had just bit into my chicken sandwich when she brought up the cracked nipples. I shot her a look. "I'm not there yet, and even just saying cracked nipples makes me want to toss my cookies. Not to mention I'm probably never going to get that image of your boobs out of my mind. If I do have a baby, I am not breastfeeding. I learn lessons from you."

"Sorry." Brynne's cheeks colored slightly. "I got a little ahead of myself."

I waved a hand. "It's okay. And I promise to tell you the second I get pregnant – after Trent, of course."

"Man, to even think about you knocked up is just exciting."

"What about you and Aaron? Are you still trying?"

A cloud passed through Brynne's face, but as suddenly as it appeared it was gone. "Oh, sometimes. I mean, yes we have sex and everything, but we aren't trying real hard or getting real concerned about it or anything. Emmy Jo came along without trying, so I'm sure our second baby will too. It might be fun to be surprised again. Though I could deal without all the vomiting this time."

I tried to read between the lines to figure out what Brynne wasn't telling me. Were they having problems getting pregnant again? One would think after Emmy Jo coming from out of nowhere that Brynne would get knocked up again with Aaron just looking at her, but maybe that wasn't the case. But she clearly didn't want to talk about it yet, and I wouldn't push it. Brynne would come around when she was ready.

After Brynne left the store, I started to get restless. I didn't want my thoughts to wander to Trent so I started browsing the internet, looking up places I wanted to visit when we went to New York. Eventually though, my mind went right to Trent and what he could possibly be up to.

I didn't always have problems with my husband, especially not in the beginning of our marriage. I thought he was the perfect man—good looking, driven, successful, attentive, good in bed. If I had to put my finger on when I starting noticing a change I would say last year, maybe a bit before. And I couldn't really explain what that change even was. He was still attentive to me, sent me flowers at the store for no reason, opened car doors for me, but it was like he had gotten...sleazy. All these little sex comments would be made, he started asking me often to send him "naughty" picture messages, he wanted to be more adventurous in the bedroom. I thought maybe he was just getting bored with our married life already, which terrified me. I didn't want a divorce, especially so soon after tying the knot. I went along with his requests to make him happy, but I wasn't making myself happy in the process.

But besides those little factors, there weren't any other significant changes I could put my finger on. It was just a feeling, women's intuition. But now with what I found in his office...it seemed my feelings were pretty freaking accurate.

Opening up photos of Time Square, I thought again about telling Brynne what I had found. I just didn't want to worry my friend. Brynne was the mothering type, and I knew she would only worry herself if I told her. And it wasn't like I was lying to my friend about anything – I truly didn't know yet what was going on. I never mentioned the slight shift in Trent's behavior that I had been noticing. I knew Brynne thought we were a perfect couple, and I was ashamed to admit that sometimes I played that up. No one has a perfect relationship and Brynne should know that, but I could be known to exaggerate from time to time. Not because I was trying to make us seem better than anyone, I just wanted Brynne to believe I was beyond happy. She had kept a close eye on me since we became roommates in college, and I knew she wanted me to be happy more than anything.

And it wasn't like I was unhappy. I gave my head a shake, trying to get these thoughts out of my mind. I was supposed to be researching our trip, or closing the shop, or doing something rather than wallowing by myself. I stood and closed the internet browser, preparing to start the closing duties.

My thoughts were still a bit all over the place when I pulled up to The Window, a fancy restaurant on the edge of town that looked over the beach. All sides of the establishment were massive windows so you could enjoy the scenery no matter where you were seated, and the hostess's wore black dresses and the waiters donned tuxedos. I didn't have time to go home and change – nor did I want to drive fifteen minutes in the opposite direction to our house and then turn around and come back to town – so I felt slightly underdressed in my black slacks and blue button up work shirt. At least I found a pair of black heels in the back seat that I slipped on, and was carrying a smaller Prada bag today instead of my bulky Michael Kors one.

The hostess greeted me by name and showed me to the table where Trent was king of the court. There were two other men and their wives there, all listening with rapt interest as Trent discussed a piece of workout equipment they had on order. I slipped into an empty chair to the right of Trent (who was manning the head of the table, of course) and set my purse by my feet, not interrupting. It was like nothing had happened though, as Trent didn't stop speaking and not one eye flicked in my direction.

I picked up the glass of white wine in front of me that Trent had been thoughtful enough to order and took a sip. Pinot Grigio. Not my favorite since I liked sweeter wines, but it would do.

"It's simple to use, the abs get a great workout, and it's a smaller piece of equipment that won't take up a lot of space. I have three pieces being sent to Onakat and three to Gimbley and we'll see how they take to it. If we get the positive feedback I can almost guarantee will come our way, I want at least three pieces in all the gyms by summer." Trent finished up his spiel and leaned back in his chair, taking a swig from his glass (probably whisky sour) and looking quite proud of himself. That flicker of pride rose inside me before I could think twice about it. He loved his career, and I was happy for him.

"Honey, so glad you could make it down." He finally turned his attention to me, giving me a kiss on the cheek. "You remember Dan and Jim, right? And their lovely wives Katrina and Kimberly."

"Yes, of course. Hello, everyone. Nice to see you all again." Katrina and Kimberly were best friends and looked alike in that snobby housewife-who-lives-off-their husband look. Smooth dark hair down their back, always a face looking too heavily made-up, lots of diamonds and jewelry dripping everywhere, and designer labels on everything they wore. Sometimes I thought Trent wanted me to look more like them, but I didn't find their look attractive in the least. It seemed more painful and time consuming to me than anything. I knew he was probably really disapproving of my outfit tonight, especially compared to the slinky dresses the K's were wearing, but I knew he wouldn't mention I was working – he didn't believe I should hold a job when he was the supporter.

"Glad you could make it down. Real busy tonight, Portland?" Katrina aimed for what I believed was to be a smile, but the (alleged) Botox was giving her a tough time letting her smile and look concerned at the same time.

Trent reached down and set his hand on my knee. I knew he wasn't being sweet, it was a reminder not to talk about EJ Reads. "Oh, yes. I had to pop over to a friend's house and watch her daughter for a bit while she worked. I came straight here from their house. So sorry about my clothes. Can't wear a nice outfit around a three year old!"

Polite chuckles could be heard around the table, and Trent visibly relaxed.

"That's a shame your friend still has to work – especially with a child at home! What does her husband do?" Kimberly looked horrified, and I felt my insides turn. I knew the incessant questions, mundane gossip, and talk about price tags was going to be my night. Joy.

"He owns his own company. He's actually quite successful. She owns her own business as well, so they are just busy bees over there!" I tried to make light of the conversation, but feared me finishing the glass of wine in a few gulps gave away my discomfort.

"I just don't see why one would want to take on owning a company when their husband can handle all of that. I would want to stay home with my children," Kimberly said.

And the nanny, I added as a silent afterthought. "Oh, are you thinking about having a baby?" I asked instead, trying to keep my eyelids from snapping shut thanks to this beyond boring conversation.

Kimberly gave a throaty laugh. "Not quite yet. I'm in the best shape of my life right now thanks to my lovely husband. I wouldn't want to ruin it with a baby bod." She winked at Jim, who openly scanned her body before winking back. Sick.

I nodded, raising my glass at the waiter who was passing by. This was going to be a long night.

Around eleven, our group finally seemed to wind down and checks were delivered. I was about three sheets to the wind with all the wine I consumed on an early-dinner stomach. It helped take the edge off, and I might even say I enjoyed some of the conversations

I had with Katrina and Kimberly. I still wanted to peel my own eyeballs at some of the things they said, but I managed to make it through without maiming myself.

"Gentlemen, thanks for having dinner with us tonight. I'll be heading out of town come Monday, but email me the latest figures by Wednesday and I'll be sure to go through them," Trent said, shaking hands with Dan and Jim and kissing Katrina and Kimberly on the cheeks.

We were off shortly after, with Katrina calling after me promising to send me the number of her facialist – my eyeballs were seriously endangered at that point. I pretended as though I hadn't heard her and continued on, concentrating on putting one foot in front of the other and not stumbling out of the restaurant.

Once outside, the cool salty breeze made me feel better, and I relaxed into Trent. He kissed the top of my head, and I could almost feel myself slipping into the area where I believed nothing was wrong. My husband was my husband, and he loved me.

"Let's take the cab home, honey," he said then, leading me towards a waiting taxi that he must have had the hostess call from inside the restaurant. "Good thing Dan picked me up tonight. Maybe Brynne can give you a ride in the morning to pick up the BMW."

"Yeah. Brynne. I have to go the gym tomorrow with Brynne. Brynne will pick me up," I said, trying not to sound as drunk as I felt.

"Here we go." Trent opened the taxi door for me and I slid inside, wanting to fall asleep the minute my ass hit the seat.

Trent slid in behind me and gave our address to the driver, who was off. I leaned my head against Trent's chest and concentrated on not throwing up on his shoes.

CHAPTER 5

Brynne

"I brought coffee." I held out a cup to Portland as she poured herself into the car, sunglasses in place and a black knit cap covering her hair.

"Thanks," she grunted, reaching for the cup and taking a sip. "I feel like shit."

"What happened last night?" I pulled out of her driveway and headed for the gym. I'd been a little surprised when Trent texted late last night asking if I could pick up Portland before going to the gym, saying she had to leave her car at The Window. Portland and I both enjoyed our cocktails, but very seldom did we get drunk-drunk. And from the looks of Portland leaning her forehead on the cold glass window, she had gotten drunk-drunk the night before.

"Ugh, it's just those people Trent insists on being around for work. And their snobby wives in their designer clothes with all the body fat sucked out of them and their Botoxed frozen faces. Being around them makes me feel like I'm back in the '50's or something, where men brought home the bacon and the wife just looks pretty with a blank look on her face all day while vacuuming in heels. Except these wives don't even have to vacuum anymore, they hire out for that."

I took a left turn to head into town, listening patiently to Portland get it all out.

"But enough about me. Really. They're nice people, we just don't see eye to eye on everything. How was your Friday night?"

"Just about as wild and crazy as ever. I made dinner, Aaron showed me some designs, Emmy Jo watched a movie, and then we went to bed early. I didn't see the text from Trent until this morning."

"I'm glad he texted you, because I would have completely forgotten and either missed the gym or made you drive to my place all the way from the gym."

I nodded, thinking about Trent and what a devoted husband he was.

"Sorry anyway that you had to come get me. And then slug me over to The Window afterwards. I just about forgot the car keys on my way out. That would have been a disaster." Portland slumped in her seat and tilted her head into her hands.

I looked over at her, concerned. "Everything all right? You know it's not a big deal for me. Not at all."

"I know. But now I feel bad complaining about those wives. They are nice people, really."

"P, you don't have to be best friends with them just because Trent works with their husbands. I'm sure you were plenty polite and nice to them last night, and that's all that matters."

"You're right. You're right, I should stop beating myself up over it. Moving on now."

"Good."

"Did I tell you my dad is coming up next weekend?"

"No! When did you find that out?" I loved Portland's dad, and I knew it made her happy when he came for a visit.

"He's been emailing me off and on about it but I told him yesterday about Trent being gone for so long and tried to play the lonely card. I checked my email this morning and he replied saying he is going to come up on Saturday for the day and spend the night before heading back on Sunday."

"Sounds terrific! Is he still seeing that woman – Darlene?"

"He hasn't mentioned her a whole lot lately, but I would think he would tell me if he wasn't."

"Do you think maybe you'll meet her soon then? Around Easter maybe?"

Portland shrugged. "Not sure. Maybe."

I pulled into the gym parking lot and within no time we were running side by side on the treadmills. While we typically frequented the gym together at least twice a week we were more meticulous about it lately, as we were running a 5K just next week and wanted to be prepared. My thoughts drifted from crossing the finish line to Portland's father, happy he was coming for a visit, and wondering if he would mention anything about this Darlene and if the relationship was serious. I wondered how Portland would take the news if it was. I honestly thought she would be fine – probably even happy for her dad – but I didn't know that for sure. Even though Portland was my best friend, she was hard to read sometimes.

Portland's mom died when she was nine years old. It was a story that made me sick every time I had to think about, tell the story, or relive it with Portland when we had a moment of silence on October ninth every year. Portland's mom was a drug addict, and that addiction eventually took her life. Jim, Portland's dad, filled in the blanks for me one night when I was staying at their house on a weekend visit in college.

"She doesn't like to talk about that much, does she?" he had asked me as we were sitting on their porch, looking up at the stars. Portland had just stormed inside the house moments earlier after Jim mentioned visiting Laurie's grave before we headed back to campus.

"I know she passed away. Portland said it – it was drugs?" I faltered over my words. I had never really known a world of drugs existed. I saw things about it on TV and with celebrities, but no one around me did drugs. My parents didn't even smoke cigarettes. The first time I got offered pot at a college party I thought it was a regular cigarette, and even considered taking a drag before coming to my senses.

"It was. My Laurie – she tried to get help many times. It just never seemed to stick. She wasn't into all that when we were married. She had gotten mixed up in a bad crowd in her younger days, but when I met her at nineteen she was clean as a whistle and even told me about entering rehab when she was sixteen, on a court order. Did that make me a little scared of her? Sure. But I loved her with all my heart, and I believed her one hundred percent when she told me she was off that stuff for good.

"And then we had little Portland and her life – it was just never the same. They call it post-partum depression now, but we just called it baby blues back then. Portland gave her the baby blues. Funny what an opposite effect she had on me. She lit up my life – still does. I thought I loved Laurie with all my heart but when Portland came, I loved her with all my soul. But Laurie just couldn't seem to get it right. She got upset over the smallest things, and Portland crying nearly made her want to jump out the window. But over time, she got better. I thought it had just gone away, like the doctors said it would."

He had smiled softly, and I remembered gripping my hands together, wondering what he would say next. Portland hadn't mentioned any of this to me.

"But it turns out she wasn't just better on her own, she had started getting outside help. First alcohol, then back to the drugs. Portland was damn near three years old by the time I figured it out. How stupid I was." He laughed bitterly, and I noticed then how much he seemed to age right before my very eyes. It scared me, saddened me.

"We fought like crazy over it. I wanted to protect Portland, protect Laurie, protect my home. I won't hurt your young ears repeating some of the stories Laurie told me about her youth days and drugs and what she did for them – and what they did to her when she couldn't pay them back."

A chill had run down my spine. I couldn't even begin to imagine what he could be talking about – I was still so naïve back in those days.

"I wanted to leave her so bad. I wanted to get Portland and run, not wanting to mix up my innocent daughter in what Laurie had going on. But I loved her. I wanted her to get better. I wanted to help her. So I stayed. I tried my hardest not to be an enabler. I showed no mercy when she was sick, I got her into a rehab program a few times, I threw away her drugs and pills whenever I found them – but she always found a way to get more. Always."

I had swallowed hard, knowing something big was about to be revealed to me.

"She wasn't on drugs straight throughout the years. There were times where she got off for a while, usually after the rehab programs. But she went back and was never able to shake it." Jim had looked off into the night, into the darkness of the trees. "She died when Portland was nine, of a heroin overdose. And Portland – my little, sweet Portland – was the one who found her in bed."

I had gasped, trying to cover my mouth but it was too little too late. Jim looked over at me and blinked, as if he had forgotten I was still there.

"Yes, it was awful. The worst moment in my life, a moment that will haunt me to my grave. Portland came screaming into the backyard. I was just a few feet away from here, working on sanding some wood. She was screaming something was wrong with Mommy, she wasn't waking up. I dropped all my tools and ran, but it was too late."

I had wiped away a few tears that had begun to fall, my heart aching for my friend and her still grieving father. There was a lot of unfairness in this world, but for a little girl to discover her own mother's body? The injustice paralyzed me.

Jim had looked me right in the eyes; I saw the haunted look clear as day. He felt like he had failed his daughter in some way. I wanted to hug him then, to let him know how much Portland talked him up to me, how much her love for her father was obvious, even after what they had been through. But the story had taken my voice away and I just stared back, hurting for this man.

Portland didn't return outside for almost an hour that night, and the story of her mother wasn't brought up again until almost a full year later when Portland and I spent the night together and she finally opened up to me after about four glasses of wine. I toed the line delicately when I told her what I knew, and all she had done was nodded, patted my hand, and say she was tired. Over the years she had finally come to talk about it more, eventually telling me in vivid detail about that horrific day and her discovery, what she felt during the funeral, and how she visited her mother's grave only once each year, on the anniversary of her death. I started accompanying her back to her hometown and the cemetery each October since we moved to Delany.

Portland had been my best friend for seven years, but I could still feel a disconnect at times when it came to her mom and her past. I knew that she didn't want me to worry for her, but that was impossible. I loved Portland, and I knew she deserved happiness in life.

That was why I was overjoyed when she met Trent. He was just the man she needed. He loved her, practically worshipped the ground she walked on. When Portland said she wanted something, he made sure she got it. His gifts to her were extravagant but also thoughtful. The love they had for each other was special, and she deserved every last piece.

"I can't run anymore. I think I'm going to try the bike for a bit." Portland turned off the treadmill and wiped her face with a towel. "You going to run for much more?"

"Actually, I'm going to pop into the bathroom quick. I'll meet you by the bikes when I get back."

She nodded and I slowed the treadmill down to a walk, then hopped off and headed out of the room towards the restrooms in the back of the gym. I tried to keep my walk casual, but I really wanted to sprint to the bathrooms.

I pushed open the heavy door and quickly took a seat. While I didn't need to go to the bathroom, I wanted to be off my feet for a minute and try to let the cramps subside. I leaned my head against the cool stall door, trying not to think about germs. My stomach was twisting and turning so bad I felt like someone was pushing barbed wired into my skin. I was sweating, and not just from the workout, but from the pain.

I hadn't told anyone about the cramps yet, not Portland or even Aaron. They had started coming on just last week, and at first I chalked it up to period pain. I thought it was strange since I wasn't one to suffer from cramps all that much, but sometimes I would get a passing cramp on the first day or two of my period. But the cramps were lingering and much more painful than they ever had been. I was also on day eight of my period, which was odd as well. For as long as I could remember I had been on a five day period schedule, so day six was weird but I didn't worry, day seven I was confused and slightly worried, but day eight...I didn't know what to think. I actually wondered for a brief moment if I was pregnant, only to realize that duh – periods usually symbolized otherwise. I was just so excited and looking for a happy excuse to explain my body, but now I wondered if something could be really wrong.

I slowly peeled down my pants and underwear. Heavy blood. I

exited the stall and grabbed a tampon out of the basket of freebies by the sink. That was another thing that was off-kilter. Not only were my periods five days, but I was a light bleeder. I had no idea where all this heavy stuff was coming from, but that was causing me to be even more scared. I knew I should schedule a doctor appointment, but what if...

Stop that, I told myself firmly. I finished up in the bathroom and washed my hands, looking at myself sternly in the mirror. Nothing was wrong, and even if it was, I couldn't be stupid about it. I couldn't just put off a doctor's appointment because I was afraid of bad news. I'd heard too many stories of women that find a lump in their breast but convince themselves nothing is wrong, only to put it off and then get diagnosed with stage 4 breast cancer because they were too busy trying to fool themselves. If something was wrong, hopefully I was going to catch it early enough. It was only the third day of my body giving me a sign. I had time to make the appointment.

I headed back to the cardio room and took a seat at the empty bike next to Portland. "What do you have going on the rest of the day?" I asked as I started pedaling, trying to push any scary thoughts of cancer or sickness out of my head.

"Just getting the car really. Thought about doing some house cleaning so it's not in terrible shape for when Dad comes. How about you?"

"I'm going to pop into EJs in the afternoon and help Serena close up. Then we have an appointment with the accountant to go over our final tax preparations. We are seriously behind there and I'm started to get worried. But I think they only need our signatures now and then they can file it. Finally!"

"I'm just glad I don't really have any part of that. I just hand Trent my W-2 from EJs and his accountant takes care of all of it. I know Trent is more involved with all the write-offs and junk he has to do and keep track of, but I'm glad I'm out of that!"

"Amen! I think next year will go a lot smoother as we get more used to both being self-employed. And hopefully we get some money back this year. We had to pay in last year with just Aaron's self-employment tax, but we did the estimated tax thing this year and hopefully that helped. It probably won't be much, but we can put it towards our New York trip or something!" We weren't hurting financially by any stretch of the imagination, but it was always nice to get some extra money and not pay even more into the government if you didn't have to.

"I was looking at some places online last night too and I'm getting a list together of things I want to see. Hopefully we have enough time to cover everything!" Portland said.

"I hope so too! And the guys cannot complain about us taking a day to shop since we're going to the game with them. We deserve it!"

"Agreed! Hopefully we can pencil in a date soon."

"I think Aaron said the team schedules are out but they just have to look at their work calendars and decide which date will be best. I'll get on him some more to get one picked so we can have that done and over with."

We finished up on the bikes, did some light stretching, and headed out the doors. After dropping Portland off at The Window and saying our good-byes, I pointed the Tucson home. I pulled out my cell phone while at the stoplights on 92nd and hovered my finger over my OB-GYN's office number. Figuring it was a Saturday and the offices might be closed, I put my phone back in my purse and continued driving. I'd call Monday.

CHAPTER 6

Portland

"That's great, Dad. I'm excited to meet her. No, I'm being honest. I'm really excited to meet Darlene. Of course we have enough room, is that even a real question? Okay. See you soon. Bye."

I hung up the phone and placed it on the kitchen counter, drumming my nails on the granite. Dad was bringing his girlfriend back to Delany for a visit. It was like a meet-the-parents scenario, except reversed. I shot off a text to both Brynne and Trent with the news. I wasn't sure what Trent's reaction would be since we didn't talk a lot about Darlene and my thoughts on Dad having a girlfriend, but I was sure Brynne would be thrilled.

Ding. Sure enough. *Brynne Ropert: Wow, that's amazing! So exciting you get to meet her! Let's go out for dinner one of those nights!*

I thumbed back a reply, trying to sound as enthusiastic as my friend. It wasn't that I wasn't excited for my dad, it was just ... weird. I had met a few casual acquaintances of my dad's since Mom died, but no one had lasted as long as Darlene or seemed as serious. I think after I was fourteen and had a little incident with one of Dad's friends (I remember shouting "Whore" at her at one point – I was fourteen and just started my period, cut me some slack) that he toned down the dating and focused solely on work and putting me through school. I hadn't met another "friend" of his since that unfortunate incident and I'd never heard him call a woman his girlfriend since then either. This was going to be a big step, and I needed to get over my weird feelings.

I had been Trent-less for just over twelve hours, yet I hadn't stepped foot into his office yet. I ran errands in town after work, washed the car, cleaned the house, made a light dinner, and now...it was approaching eight at night and the thoughts of searching were consuming me. I tried to see if Brynne wanted to join me for a night in at home, but she was preparing for EJ's field trip the next day. It was just me and my thoughts. Always dangerous.

I stepped out of the kitchen and found my feet leading me to Trent's office, even though my mind was trying to say something otherwise. *Go out! Go to Brynne's! Go to freaking bed!* But no, I was now sitting in Trent's office chair, firing up his laptop that stayed at home. I would hit up the desktop after.

The password page popped up, and I quickly typed in tp0518 – our first initials and wedding date. I held my breath, but the home screen popped up like normal. Clearly Trent couldn't be hiding anything, because wouldn't he have changed the passwords? That would only make sense.

While the icons were loading, I willed myself to stand on the chair, once again being able to look at the top of his desk. The papers were there, the folders were there, the calendars were there. It didn't appear anything had been moved from my last visit. I didn't know whether to feel relieved or terrified. If Trent had something going on in his life on the side, wouldn't he be better at hiding stuff than just the top of his desk? A thought sickened me. Unless he thought I was too trusting, too trusting to go snooping about. Too dumb to put two and two together. Yes, I didn't talk about my mom much, but he knew she died of a drug overdose. I didn't go into the specifics or talk about how much I researched all the drugs she did, the effects they had one one's body, etc., but I was well informed on a lot of things when it came to drugs.

I grabbed the paper on the top of one file, the paper that had landed in front of me last week when I was innocently looking for tax papers. It was a list, almost like an inventory sheet. At the top was typed "Rock." The paper was divided into two separate columns. One had measurements and either a name or phone number next to it, the other column had locations, also along with a name or phone number. The first column had measurements in kilograms, the second column had measurements in grams. Flipping the paper over, I saw the back side had the same setup, except this one was labeled "Powder." Same column set-up, different names, numbers, locations, and measurements.

I sat heavily on the office chair, staring at the paper. When did my husband become interested in drugs? Who the hell was getting him kilos of cocaine, and why did it appear he was then selling that?

Cocaine has two different forms, powder or crack. Powder – or coke or blow on the streets – is snorted or injected by users. Crack – also known as rock – is smoked. When someone sells cocaine on the streets it is typically measured in grams, which is what the second column on this paper was indicating. When someone is smuggling cocaine, that is done in large amounts, often measured in kilograms. That explained the first column. But nothing explained what the hell I was looking at. A cocaine schedule? Drop-off and pickup times and names and numbers and amounts all swam before my eyes. There was no way Trent could be involved in drugs. He wasn't on drugs – I surely would be able to tell. Sometimes he traveled for days or weeks at a time but if someone was using drugs even sporadically, I would know. And they would crave it, become addicted. It wasn't possible Trent was actually under the influence.

But was he selling them? Did he have a side business going on?

Who the hell and what the hell was he mixed up in? And how in the world did I go about asking him?

I got back on the computer next, my body and brain both feeling on auto-pilot. I was a woman on a mission. I had watched drugs destroy my mother's life – and not just hers. Her addictions and overdose took so much out of my dad, who tried everything he could to help her get clean. And I lost my mother when I was nine. Nine years old. I had to find her lifeless in bed. I touched her arms, her face, her hair. I put my head down to her chest to see if I could hear a heartbeat, like I had seen in the medical shows my parents would watch together. Before running to get my dad, I stood over my mom's body. I didn't cry, I didn't yell. I just looked at her. Her blonde hair was in waves on the pillow and her face was pale. Mom never had the best skin (because of the drugs of course) but you only really saw that when she slept and didn't have all her makeup on. I remember standing back and looking at her body and thinking to myself *Mother, what have you done now? How could you do this to me?*

She left me when I was a kid. No one took her from me. She didn't have a freak accident or cancer. She did this to herself, and she did this to me. I had to make it through school on my own. I had to make it through puberty, training bras, and tampons on my own. I had to make it through homecomings and proms and other first dates on my own. My dad tried hard, but those first years after she passed were pure hell for him. He put a lot of the blame on himself, I understood that now. Not just for Mom's drug use, but for keeping me around her. I knew that he could never forgive himself for having me be the one who found her. We struggled for so many years, father and daughter, trying to figure out how to make it in this world. I hate when I say I had to go through things alone when he tried so hard, but it was simply never the same. A girl should have her mother. And she let herself go.

As I scrolled through files on the computer, trying desperately to find any more information that I could, my mind flashed back to our wedding day. I didn't want anything that would remind me of my mother at my wedding. She loved roses, I carried peonies. She loved princesses (Disney and royalty), I requested to only try on non-ball gown dresses, and settled on a sheath dress perfect for our beach ceremony. Mom loved candles, always taking bubble baths with candles surrounding the tub and lighting candles with special dinners; I demanded no candles at the reception.

Did I still carry a grudge against my mother? Yes. Sure, I visited her grave every year, but only once a year, on the anniversary of her death. I always thought that maybe this will be the year I find it in my heart to forgive, but it never happens. I always get angry when I think about her. Will I ever stop? Honestly, I hope so. Who carries a grudge against their dead mother for sixteen-plus years?

My husband was well aware of these feelings. It took some time for me to finally break down the walls I had built when I first started dating Trent. I told him in passing on our first date that my mother was deceased, but I didn't go into further details and he didn't press. It wasn't until after we were married that I finally was able to really delve into my thoughts and feelings of abandonment and betrayal. Trent would hold me, stroke my hair, tell me how much he loved me and how his wife was so brave. I was upfront about drug use – I didn't do it, I didn't like it, I didn't want to be around people who were on drugs. He knew that. He knew that about me. Why, please someone tell me why, was I finding a drug drop-off schedule in his work files?

I couldn't find anything on the laptop. No funny looking emails, documents, spreadsheets, videos. I went through the browser history––nothing. Trent and I were an open couple – we let each other know our passwords for computers, emails, Facebook, everything. We had nothing to hide from each other. How could Trent possibly be involved in something sinister when I had access to everything?

I shut down the laptop and moved on to the desktop. The password screen popped up. I typed in tp0518. I blinked in surprise at the screen, which was telling me I had entered the wrong password. I typed once again, tapping the keys slowly. tp0518. Wrong password. One more time. Wrong password. I tried pt0518. tp518. Portland0518. TandP0518. Wrong password.

I leaned back in the chair, my heart about ready to burst out of my chest. Why would the desktop computer have a different password? The desktop always had the same password. I drummed my fingers on the keys, watching the password box get filled with gibberish. I slammed my hand down on the desk. "Fuck!" I cried, startling myself. I hadn't meant to scream. I hadn't meant to lose control.

I gave up on the computers and crawled back up on the office chair, leaning over to see the top of Trent's desk. I grabbed one of the calendars I had seen last week, flipping it to today's date. Scribbled in said Canpart, which was indeed the town Trent told me he would be in. But underneath were the names Elisha Borzo and Johnny Manaco. I flipped to the drug schedule in my hands. Both Elisha and Johnny's name were on there. Elisha's only had a phone number, Johnny's had a number and an address.

After hours of being in the office, I gave up. Every bone in my body was exhausted, and I practically had to crawl to the bathroom. The only items I found in Trent's office that didn't belong to the man I married were the drug schedule and calendar that matched up with the drug schedule. Everything else was clean – work schedules, documents on equipment, an employee rolodex.

I slapped on moisturizer, barely registering the cool feeling on my flushed cheeks. Was my husband keeping something from me? If I had found files full of drug deals, I would believe it. If I had found emails backing it up, I would believe it. If I had found web pages pertaining to drugs and how to deal them, I would believe it. But one sheet of paper, one calendar? How could I know if they were even Trent's? Maybe an employee was doing something on the side and somehow the files got put into Trent's briefcase. It could be Jim – he looked like he could have been high the night at The Window. I shook my head. I was stretching it. I needed to calm down.

I shuffled into the bedroom and undressed, grabbing a pair of black sweatpants and a purple workout tank top from the dresser. When Trent was home I wore sexy pajama's – mostly just teddies – but I relished my sweats on nights he was gone. I crawled into bed and threw the comforter over me. Snuggling into the pillows, I tried to think positive thoughts. It was probably a misunderstanding. Someone else's life. My husband was a good man. He might not be the best husband in the world all of the time, but who was? Possibly Brynne's husband, but no other guy. Trent would not be into the drug scene. Not if he wanted to stay married to me, and I firmly believed that he did. He wouldn't pick drugs over me.

ॐ

I woke up the next morning feeling mildly better. I didn't have any dreams that I could remember and I had slept through the night, something I thought would not happen. After getting ready for the day and making some coffee, I rushed out of the house and climbed into the BMW. I was opening EJs that morning as Brynne whisked off with Emmy Jo's class to the aquarium. Lucky. I wished I was going to the aquarium that day.

My phone rang, and I hit the hands-free. "Hello?"

"Port. How are you, babe?" Trent.

"I'm fine. Driving to EJs. Glad you could call." I kept my voice level and smooth. There was nothing to be concerned about.

"I remembered you saying you were going to be at the store most of the day and I'm going to take a few of the managers out tonight up here, so I might not be able to call later."

"That sounds fun. Do you know the managers well?" I wondered if Elisha or Johnny's name would get brought up.

"Not real well, but hopefully that will change tonight. Everyone seems like nice people."

"That's good." I paused, trying to figure out what to say next. I was never at a loss of words around Trent, but my mind was buzzing in eight thousand directions, making it hard for me to concentrate.

"Yeah, should be good. Are you looking forward to your dad's visit?"

"Yes! I really am. I think it's about time I met Darlene."

"Really? I thought you might be nervous about it."

"Yeah. No I am nervous too, but I'm excited. I hope it's not awkward or anything. It feels like such a meet-the-parents scenario, except the daughter is meeting the girlfriend. It's just weird. And now I feel like all this pressure on me to make sure the house is in good shape and ––"

"Put that over there. No, there. Yeah, okay. Sorry, babe, had to give direction. They already have me working hard this morning. What were you saying?"

"I'm just nervous. We're going to have dinner with the Ropert's Saturday night so I won't have to worry about making a big dinner at all which is good, but––"

"Port, I'm sorry to cut you off again, but these idiots really need my help. I'll text you later, okay?"

"Oh, um, okay. That's fine. Good luck," I said, trying to swallow back a lump. I really wanted to talk to Trent, to show myself that he was normal and not hiding anything from me. I didn't want to be rushed off the phone with him.

"I'll text you later, babe. Promise. Maybe in the meantime you could send me a little sexy text, eh?"

I bit down on my lip. And we were back to that. "I don't know, Trent. What if one of your employees saw it or I sent it to the wrong person or accidently uploaded it to Facebook or something? It's too risky these days." And I hated doing it. It felt gross.

"Come on, babe. I don't get to see you for two whole weeks. A guy's got to have something to keep him going."

"Fine. If you're lucky," I said, just wanting to get out of the conversation.

"That's my girl." I hated when Trent said that; it made me feel like a dog. "Have a good day. Love you."

"Love you too." The phone disconnected and the car was quiet once again. Minutes later, I pulled into the parking lot and made my way to the door. I stepped inside the quiet bookstore, heading to the front desk. Setting my purse on the counter, I grabbed my cell phone and quickly unbuttoned my top, taking a picture of my bare breasts but making sure to keep my face out of it. I sent the text off to Trent, deleted the picture, buttoned my shirt back up, and clicked the computer on. It was time to work.

CHAPTER 7

Brynne

"Emmy Jo! Wake up, princess. Time for a field trip!" I leaned over my sleeping daughter and planted a soft kiss on her forehead. She looked like such an angel when she slept, and sometimes I hated to wake her because I just wanted to continuing looking at her. But I knew there was no time for that this morning. I loathed being late to any school functions.

"Mmm," Emmy Jo mumbled and stretched, slowly coming to.

"Come on, baby girl. Time to get up." I pushed her soft brown hair away from her face as she opened her eyes.

"MOM! It's field trip day!" she practically shouted, causing me to snap my head back. And she was up.

The next few minutes flew by in a hurry, as EJ threw her covers back and raced into the bathroom. I followed, helping her go to the bathroom (she could do it on her own, but mornings or late-night trips were always better if I was there), teeth-brushing, and getting her changed. EJ loved all things girl and princess, but somehow frilly clothes weren't a big deal to her. She had wanted to pick out her outfit the night before – she usually let me on regular school days – but still her outfit was only a pair of jeans with pink sparkles on the sides and fairly plain white T-shirt with matching pink sparkles. I ran a comb through her hair but she refused any bows or a headband, and we headed upstairs and into the kitchen.

Aaron was making eggs at the stove, a job I was grateful he took on that morning. He slid a plate of scrambled eggs and toast my way and I hungrily took my first bites, pausing to kiss his cheek. "Morning, baby," he said, kissing me back. "And good morning, princess. Are you excited for your trip today?"

Emmy Jo nodded eagerly, taking a sip of orange juice from her sippy cup Aaron handed her. "I'm going to see fish and ducks and penguins and sharks! Sharks, Daddy!" She finally took a breath and another drink, her eyes wide as she looked at us.

I held back a smile at her enthusiasm. Everything was so much... better with children. Life took on a whole new meaning once Emmy Jo came into our world. Something as small as an aquarium visit or trip to the park or even the shopping mall was completely different with her innocent eyes along for the ride. It was amazing and never failed to delight me. I know I might not have been able to have crazy fun party years since I got pregnant so young, but I was more than happy with how my life was turning out, and knew just how lucky I was to have my little girl in it.

"Sharks! You're not going to pet them, are you?" Aaron asked, taking a big bite of eggs.

"No, Daddy! You can't pet sharks – they can eat you!" Emmy Jo informed him seriously.

"Baby, eat your breakfast. We have to leave soon," I said, looking at her plate. She was working her way through her juice but barely had any foot eaten, probably from chatting with excitement.

"Well, don't get too close then," Aaron said. "What is the animal you most want to see?"

"Mmm, the penguins! I've been practicing how to walk like them." Emmy Jo scrambled down from her seat and started to penguin-walk around the kitchen. Aaron and I both burst into laughter watching our daughter, her arms straight at her sides, her feet turned out so it did indeed look like she was waddling around.

"You look just like a penguin, baby. Good job. The other penguins are going to think you're one of them!" Aaron put his breakfast eating on pause and started to wash the pots and pans.

"I can do that once we get home, babe. Eat your breakfast. I know today is a big day," I said, resting my hand on his arm. Aaron was meeting with the zoning committee for the shops on Grand. The goal was to get more information to help him build up the blueprints he would eventually submit for the bid.

"It's not much. That way you don't have to worry about them when you're home. I'm sure today is going to be a long day."

"You might be right. I know we have four adults on this trip but with thirty-two kids – that still seems like we're going to be unbalanced. I will sleep good tonight."

Aaron finished up the dishes while I ate my eggs and encouraged Emmy Jo to eat hers. After they were half gone, I deemed that acceptable and we made our way into the entryway to get into our shoes and jackets. Aaron followed us out to the car, where he strapped in Emmy Jo while I put a cooler of sandwiches and juice boxes into the trunk for our school snack later in the day.

"Bye, babe. Have a great day with the kids." Aaron stopped at the window which I had rolled down and leaned in for a kiss. "Shoot me a text when you get home. I'm just going to stay in the office until around five or so to get as much done as I can."

"Okay, I will. Have a good day and don't work too hard." I gave him another kiss before rolling up the window and backing out. Emmy Jo and I gave a final wave before the garage door closed and we drove to the school, Emmy Jo chattering the whole way about how excited she was.

I pulled into the drop-off area first to let Emmy Jo out. Miss Amanda's attendant Amber came over and got Emmy Jo, and I went to park the car in the lot. We weren't going to leave until about nine o'clock, but myself and the other volunteer mom were going to head right to the classroom to wait.

I left the cooler in the car but grabbed my purse, locking up the Tucson and walking up the sidewalk. The weather was getting warmer each day but a brisk wind still blew, and I pulled my coat tighter as I continued up the walk.

I entered the front doors and walked through the hallway to get to the daycare section. The door to Miss Amanda's room was open, so I walked through the threshold and scanned the room. All the kids were sitting in a circle in the middle of the room, and Miss Amanda was speaking. Juliette Mabry, the other volunteer mom, was sitting in the back on a small chair. I slipped quietly back by her, but not without a few waves from the children. I waved back and slipped into the chair, setting my purse by my feet.

"Everyone has to make sure they stay with their leader, okay?" Miss Amanda was saying. The kids all enthusiastically nodded their heads, their attention focused on their teacher – this amazing woman who was taking them to the aquarium. Emmy Jo was just as enthusiastic, her green eyes shining.

"Good morning," Juliette whispered to me. "Are you excited for the day?"

"Morning!" I whispered back, giving her a friendly smile. "I really am. Emmy Jo hasn't been able to talk about anything else for the past three days."

"Neither has Colin. I had to volunteer for this just because of the sheer enthusiasm he had at the idea. It should be a hoot today."

I smiled back as Miss Amanda began to tell the children who their leaders were. I listened closely when I heard "Mrs. Ropert" and the following kids were named off: Emmy Jo, Kaitlyn, Charlotte, Max, Guy, Izzie, Brent, and Kylar.

Juliette started whispering to me again about hoping eight kids weren't too much to handle. It sounded like a lot to me, but I also knew our groups wouldn't be separating, so hopefully it wouldn't be so bad. "Tina was supposed to be a leader too but she canceled pretty last minute. I hear there are some issues at home, if you know what I mean," she said, raising her eyebrows.

I caught her meaning and nodded back, a frown on my face. I didn't like being reminded how fast gossip could fly in schools. Juliette was a nice woman, and Aaron and I had actually had a handful of dinners with her and her husband Christopher. They lived just a few blocks east of us, and their son Colin was a cute freckle-faced boy with a loud voice. Juliette didn't work and Christopher was a mortgage lender; Colin was their only child. Sometimes Juliette could remind me of those gossipy moms who always needed to know the latest rumor, but overall I thought she was nice. I didn't think there were any of the room moms that I wouldn't be able to get along with.

Juliette and I kept up a pleasant chat about our children, work, and the upcoming 5K for cancer charity while Miss Amanda and Amber continued to talk to the children. At nine o'clock sharp Juliette and I began to pitch in, helping the children get into their jackets and outerwear. The kids formed a line by the door and with Miss Amanda leading the way, Amber following up the rear, and Juliette and I straggling in between, we marched to the front of the building. Once there, Amber and another school attendant stayed with the children while the three of us grabbed vehicles. I could take six kids in the Tucson, Juliette five in her SUV, and Miss Amanda had a rented van from the school. Another van was needed at the last minute due to Tina's cancellation, and Amber was going to drive that one. That van was already waiting at the front, and Amber started calling out names from a list for the children that would be in her vehicle.

I pulled the Tucson up to the front, right behind the van Miss Amanda would be driving. Juliette followed closely behind me. The only two kids from my group that wouldn't be in my car were Kaitlyn and Guy. I helped each of the kids get buckled in, ensured Kaitlyn and Guy were in Miss Amanda's van, and climbed into the driver's seat.

"Are we ready to see some animals?" I called out, turning around to smile at the six peaceful faces looking back at me.

"Yes!"

"Penguins!"

"I want to see the shark's teeth!"

"I want to feed the fish!"

I turned back around, smiling to myself. It was going to be a loud day.

Once there, we parked in the lot that barely had a car in it yet (opening time wasn't until ten, it was about five minutes to) and I helped the kids get unbuckled and had them stand next to the car while I helped the others out. Soon enough, Kaitlyn and Guy joined our group and the class filed into the building, stopping at the ticket office. Miss Amanda handed the lady at the booth an envelope filled with our pre-paid tickets, and each child was given a little box filled with fish food for our upcoming stop to the tank.

After all the children had their box in hand, we trekked outside once again and crossed over the footbridge to visit the duck pond. I kept a close watch on my eight kids, but got a kick out of seeing the ducks as well. "Look, Mom! Baby ducks!" Emmy Jo, said pointing to the eight babies.

"They are cute, aren't they?" I said.

"I asked my mom once if we could get a duck," Max informed me, looking at me with serious brown eyes.

"And what did she say?" I asked with a smile.

"She said no." He said it just as calmly, clearly not too concerned he didn't get a duck.

I nodded my head at the same time Emmy Jo asked, "Can we get a duck, Mom? And a baby duck?"

I decided to take my cue from Max, and said simply, "No."

Emmy Jo looked at me for a moment before responding, "Okay," and walked ahead with the rest of the group.

I shook my head as we continued walking, and realized suddenly what the next exhibit was. "Penguins!" I heard my daughter shriek, and I quickly pulled out my digital camera from my purse to capture her expression.

"These are Magellanic penguins," our guide informed us, as all the kids ran to the windows to watch. "They come from South America and are used to a climate just like Maine, so they love it here. What they love even more than the climate is when it's feeding time – which is right now!"

Delighted gasps rose from the class, and I snapped pictures while keeping a close eye on Emmy Jo. She was having the time of her life.

"In here is the North Atlantic exhibit, which features creatures that you will find right here in Maine!" Our guide was perfect, a cute old man that clearly loved kids – and animals. "The best part of this room is the touch tank. Who wants to feel a starfish?"

Thirty-two hands shot into the air. They had three touch tanks, where the children could actually put their hands in and feel starfish and sea urchins. My memory card was filling fast, and I knew the other parents would get a kick out of these pictures. It took a while, but eventually everyone got their turn and we moved along to the seal exhibit. The guide informed us they usually ate at eleven and it was just about eleven-thirty, but they held off a bit for us so the children could watch the seals enjoy their meal time as well.

Our final exhibit we visited before we broke for lunch was the tropics, which was a slim hallway with huge tanks on both sides, featuring tropical fish (some even venomous according to the guide!), lobster, and massive amounts of colorful reef.

The kids were starting to get loud and some even impatient, so it was a good time to stop and eat. We were led into a small conference room, where we passed out the sandwiches I had made the night before and the juice boxes I brought, along with apples slices and grapes from Juliette and dessert the aquarium provided – soft serve ice cream. I walked around making sure each child got their food and was eating, cleaned up spills, and helped collect garbage.

Once bathroom breaks were complete and the conference room looked back to normal, the tour started right back up. The next exhibit?

"SHARKS!" I heard the cry sound up before I could even see anything due to my spot in the back. Sure enough, it looked as though we were standing right in the shark tank.

"And this is the shark tank," our guide commented with a smile on his face. "But it's not only sharks in here. You'll also see our loggerhead sea turtle swimming by, piranhas, and if you keep walking down here past the tank, a few tropical birds."

The kids were in awe, running right up to the thick glass that separated them from the sharks and gazing at them in wonder. A cheer went up when the sea turtle indeed swam by, seemingly oblivious to the hungry sharks roaming around.

The shark exhibit was the largest, and we spent quite some time in there. It was all right, since that was the end of the tour. Around two o'clock, we were packing up the cars and heading back to the school. The kids got a little gift bag on the way out, each containing a pencil with turtles on them and erasers shaped like a shark. They were ecstatic with their new gifts, as one could imagine. My car was loud on the way back, but noticeably more subdued. Nap time was overdue for the kids, and I knew the rest of the school day was going to be a quiet one.

Sure enough, before all the kids were even back in the classroom, others were asleep on their nap mats. After ensuring everyone was out of the vehicles and back in the classroom, I went over to Emmy Jo's yellow mat and crouched beside her. She was out like a light. I gave her a quick kiss before heading up to the front of the room to say my good-bye's.

"Thank you again for coming, Mrs. Ropert. It was a pleasure having you here," Miss Amanda said. I thought Emmy Jo's teacher was fabulous, in her late twenties and someone that clearly had a knack with children. She had light blonde hair that was always wavy and sharp blue eyes. I described her personality at times as a cupcake. What did that mean? Not sure, but that's how I would describe her.

"The pleasure was all mine. I'll be sure to get these photos printed off and send them with Emmy Jo next week to pass out. I hope the parents enjoy them."

"I'm sure they will. That sounds wonderful. The report from the aquarium will be going home with all the kids next week, a write-up of what we did and saw, and I'm going to include quotes from a few of the kids in there as well," Miss Amanda said, tucking a curl behind her ears. "If you have a good group shot on your camera, email that over to me and I'll include it on there."

"Wonderful idea! I'm sure I have some that will be perfect." We finished up our conversations and Juliette and I walked out of the building together, back to the parking lot. We exchanged pleasantries before departing, working out a time the following week for our families to have dinner together.

I drove home, looking forward to a nap myself, even though I only had about another hour before having to pick up Emmy Jo. As I pulled into our garage and started unloading gear from the car, I paused. My doctor's appointment. I had forgotten to call and schedule it.

CHAPTER 8

Portland

"Dad! Welcome! Hi, you must be Darlene." I swung open the front door and ushered Dad and his girlfriend inside. Dad was rolling a small overnight bag behind him and Darlene had a black travel bag over one shoulder. She was also carrying a bottle of wine, which I took from her as they came into the entryway.

"So great to finally meet you, Portland. I've really been looking forward to this." I pegged Darlene to be around Dad's age, in her late fifties, with close cropped blonde hair and pale brown eyes. She wore glasses that looked stylish, and had on a cute navy trench coat. First appearances went well enough.

"Feel free to set your bags here and I'll get to them later. I have some appetizers in the kitchen and I can open this as well," I said, indicating the bottle of red Darlene had brought with her.

We made our way into the kitchen, where I had a plate of cheese, crackers, bite-sized shrimp, and a favorite of Dad's – jalapeno crab dip.

"You didn't have to go through all this trouble for us," Darlene said, as Dad immediately reached for the crackers, spreading dip between two and popping them into his mouth. Darlene smiled affectionately at him, shaking her head.

"Oh, it was no trouble. I just wasn't sure if you would be hungry and our dinner reservations aren't until 6:30. We can snack on this most of the day in case hunger pangs strike."

"Thanks, Port," Dad said, loading up another cracker.

"Go easy, Dad. I only bought one case," I quipped.

"It looks like you have a lovely home," Darlene said, looking around the kitchen.

"Oh, why don't you let me give you a tour?" I said. A tour would be a great way to pass some of the time and get more pleasantries out of the way, instead of just staring at each other from across the counter.

"Terrific! Now your dad said you had the home built just for you? That sounds pretty amazing. Was it hard work?"

"You know, it kind of was." I led them out of the kitchen and into the family room. "A lot of people think building a custom home is all great and grand and you let other people do the work, but Trent and I were involved every step of the way. We had to pick out the lot, decide what kind of house we wanted, what kind of exterior materials we wanted used, then what the inside would look like. Then when you start thinking about the inside you have to decide what type of floors, walls, even the doorknobs and light switches! It was quite a process, honestly."

"Wow. But it must be so nice to get everything you want and to know you had total control over your house."

"Oh, yes. It really was. And Trent was really excited for it."

"Do you plan on being here for a long time then?"

"Hopefully. Trent wanted this to be our forever home, and we can clearly fit kids here. I think it will be a long time before we would consider leaving it." Unless...

"That's wonderful." Darlene beamed at me, continuing to ooh and ahh over the house as we worked our through the main level and then onto the basement. I quickly bypassed over Trent's office before we headed down the steps, not wanting anything to ruin the day.

"Are you from the Springfield area, Darlene?" I asked once we were downstairs. I opened the walkout and we stepped onto the lower-level patio. Since our house was not in the city we didn't have neighbors for miles, and the land was often quiet and peaceful.

"Not originally. I grew up a northerner, in Bisby. One of my sons moved to Springfield for a job, and I eventually followed him and his wife down here to be closer to their family."

"How many children do you have?"

"Three. My boys are Mark and Matt. Mark lives in Springfield with his wife Gabby. They have three children, Joshua, Garrett, and their daughter Monica. Matt still lives in Bisby where he co-owns a resort, kind of like a bed and breakfast. A forever bachelor, that one. And Lucy lives by herself in New York, trying to take over the fashion world one assistant job at a time."

"Do you like Springfield? It's got to be different from Bisby."

"Oh, it sure is. But I like being closer to the water, too. Your dad and I like to take trips to the beach and to the amusement park."

I shot her an amused smile, and she blushed in return. "I'm sure that sounds pretty silly to you, of course."

"Not at all. That sounds nice. I'm really glad you were able to come down, Darlene." I meant that. She seemed like a great person, had a nice personality, and clearly loved my dad. What more could a daughter ask for?

"Come back inside, you crazy women. It's not summertime yet!" Dad called from inside the house. It wasn't quite cold, but neither of us had a jacket on, so we ducked back inside. I declared the tour over and we headed back upstairs. I shooed Darlene and Dad into the kitchen so I could take their bags into one of the guest rooms.

When I rejoined them, they were sitting side by side and Dad was holding up a cracker with dip in the air and goading Darlene to take a bite. She leaned forward and took a cautious bite, and Dad started laughing. He wiped a crumb from her chin and leaned in to kiss her.

I veered to the left quickly and into the bathroom, shutting the door softly behind me. I looked in the mirror, startled to see tears forming in my eyes. I was happy for my dad. He was in love, it was obvious to see. I wasn't sure if I was upset because of my mom issues, or if I was upset because of my marriage issues. But I needed to pull myself together.

ᛒᛩ

Later that evening, the three of us headed out to meet Brynne, Aaron, and Emmy Jo for dinner. We had a reservation at The Window, and I was thankful I was not going to have a repeat of my last performance there. The hostess led us back to our table, and about five minutes later the Ropert's joined us. Introductions were made, drinks ordered, and idle chit-chat began.

"Darlene, it's so great to meet you. I've been looking forward to your visit," Brynne said, bouncing Emmy Jo on her knee.

"Why thank you, Brynne. It's been a lovely visit so far. Portland has such a beautiful home, and it's been amazing getting to know her."

"Do you and Jim have Easter plans yet? If you want to come up again I'd be happy to extend the invitation. I usually host Easter at our house – just a lunch really, but we'd be happy to have you."

"I think we would love that. Last year we didn't do much of anything for the holiday, and it would be great to come up again. Maybe meet that husband of yours this time?" Darlene directed her question at me.

I set down my water glass and smiled at her. "I'm sure he would love to meet you. It's a shame he was gone so long this week. But yes, let's plan on that for Easter. I like the sound of that."

Darlene smiled at me and patted my hand. I felt a strange bond towards this woman I had met only a few hours ago. And it felt nice.

"Darlene, tell me about your family. Do you have children or grandchildren?"

And they were off, enjoying their conversation as Brynne learned about Darlene. I sat back and enjoyed the scene. Brynne and Darlene chatting, Jim and Aaron in a hot conversation about different types of wood, and Emmy Jo happily coloring a page in her coloring book while sitting on Brynne's lap. I was the odd duck out, and I wished Trent were here with us. I needed him to hold my hand and assure me all was well and no funny business was going on in his life. I hadn't let myself feel panicked yet over what I had discovered. I didn't want to believe Trent had anything to do with drugs, that my marriage might be in trouble.

"We're planning a trip to New York in the summer," I heard Brynne say, bringing my thoughts back to the table. "Maybe we can look her up and do lunch?"

I realized they must be talking about Lucy, Darlene's daughter. "You're right, B! I had forgotten all about our New York trip. Yes, you should give me her contact information and we can see if she wants to get together while we're there. I would love to meet her."

Darlene looked positively thrilled. "And I know she would love to meet you. Her schedule is always all over the place, but I'm sure with plenty of notice it won't be a problem. I'll give her a call tomorrow and remind me to leave you her email address. That's about the only way she communicates anymore."

The waiter came back to take our order and Darlene, who was sitting on my right, asked what I recommended. "I'm getting the shrimp mac'n cheese. I know it might sound childish, but it is delish. My favorite item hands down here," I said, nodding at the waiter. He scribbled it down and looked at Darlene.

"I'll have the same!" she announced, grinning at me.

I smiled back, then turned my attention to Emmy Jo. "Miss Emmy Jo, why don't you tell Darlene here about your field trip? She just went to the aquarium this week," I informed her.

"Wow, the aquarium! Did you see fish?"

"Yep!" Emmy Jo beamed.

"How about turtles?"

"We saw a big huge turtle in the shark tank!"

"Holy cow!"

"We didn't see any cows!" Emmy Jo burst into giggles, causing Brynne and I to crack up as well.

Emmy Jo proceeded to talk about her trip all the way up until the food came. The table fell quiet as everyone dug in, even Emmy Jo taking small bites of her fish sticks and abandoning her coloring for the moment.

"This is delicious, Portland! How do you not come here every week and order this?" Darlene said, closing her eyes as she shoved a forkful of noodles and shrimp into her mouth.

"Don't tell anyone, but sometimes I do! We eat here a lot for Trent's business dinners, and some nights I just stop by and grab it to go. It's my weakness."

"Mmm, mmm, no judgments here! I wonder if I could make this at home."

"Do you like to cook?" I asked, taking a sip of the wine spritzer I had ordered.

"I do. I hope my next home has a kitchen as spacious as yours. Mine now is just a small old thing and cooking can be quite difficult on ancient appliances."

"Are you – are you and Dad thinking about getting a place together?" I asked hesitantly, not sure if I wanted to know the answer. Moving in with your boyfriend was a big step – though maybe not as crazy once you were in your fifties.

Darlene glanced at Dad first, who was looking back at her. "We've started to house search a little here and there. If the right house comes along we would both be open to it."

I nodded and took another bite, processing that thought. Dad would be putting the house on the market. I was surprised he never did after Mom died – after all, who really wants to continue to live in the house where your wife died? But he always hung on to it. I assumed part of the reasoning was financial – Mom owed a lot of people a lot of money when she passed away, and that put a big strain on Dad. Him and Mom had lived in the house for years before having me, and I assumed it was paid off or well near that way at the time of her passing. Another reason I thought of was trying to continue to give me some stability in my younger years. Moving houses could have possibly meant moving school districts, and I had a lot of friends at school and in the neighborhood. I appreciated it, and I understood it was time for him to move on. With Darlene.

"That sounds great," I finally said. "If you ever need any help looking, I can come down some weekend and check out houses with you. I learned quite a bit about houses during our building process."

"That's incredible, thank you for offering!" Darlene patted my hand, her brown eyes bright. "We would love that."

"We would, Port. Thank you," Dad said. I knew he wasn't just thanking me for my offer, but for being open to Darlene and their life together.

"You're welcome, Dad."

The rest of the dinner passed smoothly, and soon enough we were eating dessert and getting our to-go boxes and checks. Emmy Jo had fallen asleep in Aaron's lap, and he carefully lifted her so she was settled on his shoulder while Brynne gathered their jackets and EJ's travel bag.

"It was wonderful meeting you," Darlene said, giving Brynne a hug. "Please be sure to let us know what we can bring to Easter. I'm looking forward to it."

"I will, Darlene. Great to meet you as well. Good luck on the house front!"

"Bye, B. I'll call you tomorrow, okay?" I said, giving her a hug. I squeezed Aaron and kissed the top of Emmy Jo's head before following Dad and Darlene out to the car.

"What wonderful friends you have, Portland. And that Emmy Jo is just the sweetest. What a bright child!" Darlene exclaimed, once we were settled in and Dad was pulling out of the parking lot.

"She really is. I'm her godmother, if I didn't tell you that," I said proudly.

"Aw, how sweet! You must spoil her rotten then."

"I really do." I grinned.

"Do you and Trent have babies on the mind yet? If that isn't too personal of a question, that is," Darlene said, glancing back at me from her spot in the front.

"Not quite yet, and no, I don't mind. With Trent's work schedule and him traveling so much he just doesn't think it's the right time yet. Hopefully in a few years work won't necessarily slow down, but that he'll be able to hire more people to make those trips for him. Then we can have a real baby discussion."

Darlene nodded, satisfied with my answer. But I wasn't. I hated still feeling that turmoil and confusion rolling around inside my belly. Would a baby fix things? If Trent was into a shady side business, would having a child snap him out of it and make him see the error of his ways? But no. If my mom had taught me anything, it was that having children wouldn't fix your problems or make anything miraculously go away.

Once we got home, Dad announced he was about half asleep and soon ambled off to the guest room. Darlene and I stayed up for a while after he left, just chatting in the kitchen. I grabbed some lemonade out of the fridge and poured us each a glass, settling into the barstool beside her at the island.

"Portland, I really can't thank you enough for this trip. Your dad – he was a little nervous about it. Almost apprehensive. He wasn't sure how you would take to me, or to us being together."

I was relieved Darlene broke the ice on that subject matter. "I could sense that he was. I wasn't always the best daughter or even person when he had girlfriends after Mom died. Of course, I was still young and trying to get over her death. But I'd like to think I've matured since then, and I am really okay with Dad dating. More than okay that he's chosen you. You guys just fit right together. I can see you make him really happy and really – that's what's most important."

Darlene smiled, looking down into her glass. "Portland, I want to ask a personal question, and you feel free to tell me straight out if it's none of my business."

I nodded, wondering where she was going with this. Back to the baby thing?

"Is everything all right with you? You and Trent?"

I was shocked. "What? Yes, of course. Everything is fine. I'm sorry, why do you ask?" I didn't think I had given anything away about what I had found in Trent's office over the course of the day and night. How could she possibly think that? Trent wasn't even here for me to act awkward around. I was baffled.

"It's just – I've been listening to you tonight. I'll ask a question and it's always Trent thinks this or Trent wants that. I've barely heard you say what you want at all. And other than me asking a question, you haven't brought up his name at all or seemed to want to talk about him. It may be nothing of course, but I have that women's intuition and I just wanted to ask."

I looked at Darlene, her face friendly and open and inviting. Should I talk to her about it? She was someone removed from the situation, not like Brynne who was so involved. Maybe it would help to talk, maybe Darlene would have an idea. But no. I couldn't put that on her, because I wouldn't want my dad to know that drugs were a possibility in Trent's life. He would kill him. And I couldn't ask Darlene to keep a secret from him; that just wasn't right.

"Wow, you do have pretty impressive skills." I managed a smile and made a snap decision. "It's not like we're having any real problems to be too concerned about, I'm just getting tired of the traveling and his crazy work schedule. I – I would like a baby. But I'm afraid I would end up like a single mother most of the time, and that's not what I want."

Darlene nodded sympathetically. "I understand, dear. What a tough spot to be in. Well, you said hopefully in a few more years he'll be able to hire more people for that type of work, right? Let's just hope you'll have that beautiful baby of your own in the next few years."

"Thanks, Darlene. That really means a lot to me. I hope so." I leaned forward on impulse and gave her a hug. I wasn't being completely truthful and that made me feel guilty, but it was better this way. I just needed some more time to figure things out.

CHAPTER 9

Brynne

Sunday night, after cleaning the kitchen and putting Emmy Jo to bed, I decided I wanted to make a dessert. Aaron poured us each a glass of wine and offered to help me. While I knew he didn't like baking, we both had a busy week and this was time to be together, to relax together. I wanted to bake to keep my mind off things. I was almost hoping Aaron would just call it a night and leave me alone, then immediately felt contrite for that thought.

"All right, what can I do?" Aaron grinned at me, his sleeves pulled up and ready to bake.

I smiled back, kissing him on the cheek before swatting his butt. "Wash your hands, please."

"Yes, ma'am. At least you know my teeth are sparkling clean. Emmy Jo was quite thorough tonight."

"Didn't want to go to bed, huh?"

"Not even a little bit." He turned the water off and looked at me. "Next direction?"

"Preheat the oven to 350 and grab some butter out of the fridge." I walked over to the cupboard and pulled out flour, sugar, and cinnamon.

"What am I helping my lovely wife bake?"

"Blueberry Buckle."

"Mmm mmm! What's the occasion?"

"No occasion really. I was going to package up a few to send with Emmy Jo for Miss Amanda and her helper Amber. The field trip was so much fun and I know that can't be easy to plan and execute, and they did a great job."

We fell silent as Aaron buttered a square glass baking dish and then added flour, sugar, and cinnamon, while I whisked more flour with baking powder and salt. Once Aaron was finished with his task, I handed him the handheld mixer so he could beat together shortening and sugar. I added an egg and milk to his mixture carefully, then poured the mixture into the glass dish.

"Can you grab the blueberries out? Top right," I said, rinsing out the large bowl and setting it in the sink to wash later.

Aaron handed me the bag and we swapped places, him going to the sink and starting to wash.

"I can do that later, honey," I said, sprinkling blueberries across the mixture, followed by cinnamon.

"I can do it, babe. This was nice of you to do. I can keep the circle going."

I placed an oven mitt over my arm – the one that looked like a lobster and cracked Emmy Jo up every time I used it – and put the dish in the oven, setting the oven timer for forty minutes.

"Let's enjoy our wine in the living room while we wait, huh?" Aaron said, handing me my glass and topping it off.

I followed him in, where he flicked on the TV to the local news station. Nothing earth shattering was on (was there ever?) and we quickly moved on to other topics.

"Portland seemed to take a liking to Darlene. What are your thoughts on that?" Aaron asked, taking a sip of white. Aaron wasn't much of a wine man, but I could get him to drink a glass of something white and light every now and again.

"I think it's great. I thought Darlene was a good woman and a good fit for Jim. I was worried about Portland but looking back, I think that was silly. She's a mature adult. She loves her dad and wants him to be happy. I think he made a good choice in Darlene."

I rested my head against Aaron's broad shoulder, feeling content. I closed my eyes in happiness, but they popped open when a cramp squeezed my stomach. I gritted my teeth, trying not to make a noise aloud. I didn't want to worry Aaron.

He didn't seem to notice as he slowly stroked my hair, his focus on the TV. The reporter was talking about the mountains and all the necessary precautions those who try to hike it must take. We watched in silence, the pain never leaving my stomach. I could feel a bead of sweat start by my hairline.

"I'm going to run to the restroom quick. I'm actually getting tired. Bedtime soon?" I asked, setting my wine glass on the coffee table and standing.

"Sure, honey. A good bedtime?" Aaron winked at me, and my spirits sank. I knew he meant sex, but my stomach was cramping so bad there was no way I could make it through any sort of sexual activity.

I gave him a weak smile and took off to the bathroom without a comment. I felt bad I hadn't told my husband yet what I was going through – or that I had a doctor's appointment scheduled for the following morning. I didn't want to prematurely worry anybody, so I kept it to myself. I mentioned in passing to Portland that I had strong period cramps, and once she noted that was unusual for me I stayed mum on the subject. I was sure there was nothing wrong, so worrying my friends and family would be unnecessary.

I noted the blood showing on the panty liner – I was going on twenty days of bleeding. While the bleeding had lightened considerably, almost like spotting, it was still there. It was getting harder and harder to tell myself nothing was wrong. And it was getting harder to ward off Aaron's advances. I rarely turned my husband down for sex, but it had been nearly a month. He hadn't outright questioned me yet, but I could sense he was wondering what the heck was wrong with me. I didn't want to say I had my period because he knew my periods only lasted a handful of days, but what could I do? I was just grateful I was finally going to the doctor, finally going to get some answers. Then I would let people know what was going on.

I came back into the living room, where Aaron was now standing and powering down the TV. We walked into the kitchen together, where I rinsed out the wine glasses. Aaron stood behind me and massaged my shoulders, leaning down to plant kisses on my neck. Sex was definitely on his mind.

I enjoyed myself for a moment, trying to let go of the thoughts that terrified me. But when Aaron's hand reached down for my breast, I forced myself to face reality. I felt bad for turning down my husband, but what other choice did I have? "I'm tired, honey. Not tonight."

I couldn't look him in the eye when he said, "Again? Brynne, is something going on? You've been tired or not feeling good for weeks now. Is – are you – are you pregnant?"

I felt my heart sink at his hopeful words. We'd been trying for so long now, of course that would be where his mind went. I was silent for an extra beat, not sure what to do or say.

"Brynne. Please tell me what's going on."

"Okay!" I hadn't meant to shout, but it came out that way. I finally met Aaron's eyes, and he looked terrified. I felt awful – what if he was wondering about an affair or something along those lines? It was selfish of me to keep this in for so long.

"There is something going on, but I wasn't sure what yet so I was trying not to worry you."

"Come on, let's sit back down." He led me back to the couch, where he pulled me onto his lap like I was the size of Emmy Jo. "Tell me, babe. I'm here for you."

"It started just around a month ago." I took a deep breath and told him all about the bleeding, the cramping, the sweating, and nausea I had been experiencing. Aaron's eyes reflected fear, but his voice remained calm.

"The doctor will see what's up, and tell us how we can make this better. Brynne, you should have told me. Here I've been working my ass off in the office not thinking twice about it, and you've been feeling like this and taking care of EJ, running the store, and the household. That's not fair to you. I could have helped."

"I'm so sorry, babe. I just didn't want anyone to worry or cause stress for anyone. It could be nothing. It could be something tiny. And I'm – I'm scared." My voice broke. "Talking about it aloud makes it seem more real."

Aaron pulled me into a hug and I wrapped my arms around his strong body, burying my head into his shoulder. The tears came hot and fast, from the pain, the unknown, and the relief at finally breaking my silence. But fear – that was atop the list.

"It will be okay, baby. It will be okay," Aaron whispered, rubbing circles on my back.

I lifted my head to meet his gaze, really wishing I could keep it together around him. I didn't want to scare him anymore than I was scared myself, because the feeling was paralyzing. Only one of us could break down at a time. Someone had to keep it together, and that clearly wasn't going to be me.

"I'm going to take off work tomorrow and come to the doctor with you," Aaron said, wiping the tears from my face.

"What? No. Aaron, that's not necessary. You need to work." I tried to protest, but he was hearing none of it.

"Work can miss me for a day. This is more important. You need someone there with you. Have you told Portland what's going on?"

I shook my head. "No. I haven't told anyone yet, not Portland or my mom. I just wanted to wait until the doctor's appointment happened so I could give them a clear idea, not have to worry them with the what-if's."

"I understand. I really do. But, Brynne, please come to me next time. I feel awful knowing this whole time you've been in pain and I've just been trying to get laid. I feel like a jackass."

"It's not your fault. You couldn't have known. And I'm sorry I hid it from you. I really am." I could see now that keeping it from Aaron wasn't the smartest. He wasn't just my husband, but my best friend and partner. He would help me through anything. It was silly of me to keep it inside.

"Come on, let's get some rest. I'll make you breakfast in the morning and drive EJ to daycare, okay?"

Tears filled my eyes once again at his words. I was so lucky. "Okay. Thank you."

The oven timer went off at that moment. We both looked towards the kitchen and then back at one another.

ß⏧

The next morning, a nervous tension enshrouded our house. To my dismay, it seemed even Emmy Jo was somehow able to feel it, because she was unusually quiet in the morning. She only took a bite of toast and refused to eat anything else. She was sullen, and I almost wondered if she was ill.

"Emmy Jo, please eat a little bit more. You're going to get sick if you don't eat," I pleaded with her, wanting to drop with exhaustion. I hadn't been able to sleep a wink last night, fear crawling all over my body like ants at a picnic. I had officially moved from thinking 'maybe nothing is wrong' to 'maybe whatever is wrong won't be so bad.' I did not have the energy to fight with Emmy Jo this morning.

"I'm not hungry! I don't want to go to school today!"

"Baby, you have to go. Mommy and Daddy have to go to work." A lie, but of course she didn't need to know that.

"You always work! I want to stay home!"

Emmy Jo was kicking her feet against the breakfast island, her little arms folded across her chest. Aaron walked in then from his shower, still rubbing a towel through his hair. I looked at him in exasperation, not sure I could deal with Emmy Jo's tantrum that day of all days. Aaron understood immediately and went to sit next to Emmy Jo, pulling her into his lap. He started talking with her calmly, asking if she would help him comb his hair and brush his teeth. One thing our daughter found hysterical was brushing our teeth. Her teeth – not so much. Our teeth – yes.

Aaron was soon leading Emmy Jo out of the kitchen, bringing her breakfast plate with him and heading into the upstairs bathroom. I leaned against the wall, closing my eyes and taking a breath. I had to get it together.

A half hour later, I was kissing a much happier Emmy Jo as Aaron loaded her into the car, and then I was alone again until he returned, pacing around the house and wringing my hands together. I did the dishes even though Aaron told me to leave them for him to do, swept the kitchen floor, and was just pulling out the Windex when I heard the garage door open.

"Honey." Aaron walked in and swiftly over to me, replacing the Windex in its proper place and putting his arms around me. "Everything's going to be okay," he whispered into my ear.

"I got you, babe," I whispered back, a line we said to one another when times were tough or one of us was feeling down.

We pulled away and I straightened my shoulders. "Ready?" Aaron nodded, and I put on a lightweight leather jacket and slipped on flats.

Forty-five minutes later, I found myself lying on the exam table, with Dr. Redfield poking around between my legs. Aaron stood by my head holding my hand. It reminded me of the scene when Emmy Jo was welcomed into the world – though much tamer and considerably quieter.

Dr. Redfield didn't talk while she worked, something I appreciated. I had doctors before her that would talk about the weather and vacations while doing their business, and I found it hard to concentrate while something was being jabbed up inside me. I much preferred the silence.

"Well, Brynne, I'll be honest with you." Dr. Redfield pulled the speculum out and rolled her chair away from me, allowing me to close my legs and relax. She popped the latex gloves off and threw them away, standing to reach the sink. As the water ran over her hands and she pumped soap into them, she said, "From my exam, I don't see anything. Nothing is jumping out at me. Of course, that doesn't mean it is nothing. With your cycle and bleeding for twenty days, something is definitely happening inside there. But hopefully – hopefully – whatever it is we are going to catch it early."

I listened to her words, trying not to get too excited for them. Because something was still wrong, she was making that clear. We just didn't know what yet. But early detection – that had to be a good thing, right?

"What's the next step, doctor?" Aaron asked, his hand still clasped in mine.

"I'll send these tests out and see what comes back. Lab results typically take around three days. From there, we'll know what the next step is. Plan on my phone call to come Wednesday. How does that sound?"

I nodded my head, rustling the paper around and sitting up. "That sounds good. Thank you for getting me in so quick."

Dr. Redfield smiled at me, coming over to stand near me and patting my shoulder. "You did the right thing calling so soon. Many women wait, sometimes just until their next pap, sometimes longer. We'll find out what this is, Brynne. Don't you worry."

I left the doctor's office feeling not good, but hopeful. I could tell from Dr. Redfield's demeanor that even though she didn't see anything from her exam, something was still there. I just had to hope we had detected whatever it was early enough. Now it was only a waiting game.

ℬℛ

Friday morning. Back in Dr. Redfield's office. Fear was gnawing at my belly. Aaron was once again by my side – or head, really – and Dr. Redfield was back between my legs. I got her phone call on Wednesday, just as she had promised.

"The pap results came back abnormal."

"Abnormal. What could be causing that?" I had asked, gripping my cell phone to my ear. I was alone in EJ Reads, thankful Portland wasn't in that day and Serena was still in school.

"Basically, it means some of the cells in your cervix don't look normal. I want you to come in for a colposcopy."

"A colonoscopy?" I was bewildered how *that* test would help with my female regions.

Dr. Redfield chuckled lightly. "Not quite. It's a *colposcopy*. I'm going to take a small sample of cells from your cervix so I can biopsy them and see if we can pinpoint the issue."

"Should I be worried?" I held my breath waiting for her answer. Dr. Redfield had been my OB for many years; I knew she would tell it to me straight.

"Not yet, Brynne. Like I said, whatever it is, we've caught it early. Let's just get some more questions answered."

I scheduled the appointment for Friday. Aaron took the news calmly, like I figured he would. He said he would take Friday afternoon off to accompany me once again.

I wasn't scared going into the appointment. I hadn't researched a colposcopy for fear of what all the internet sites would tell me. I hadn't told Portland or my parents yet what was going on, wanting to get the final answers before I started bringing other people into the story. Compared to Monday, I was really quite calm when I entered the exam room after getting weighed by the nurse. She took my vitals, then handed me two white pills and a paper cup filled with water.

"What are these?" I asked, confused.

"Just some ibuprofen. It will help with the pain after the appointment."

Maybe I should have read those pamphlets Dr. Redfield had sent home with me. Or researched online. I gulped back the pills and felt the nerves start to creep in again. Was there going to be a lot of pain? What was I getting myself into?

Dr. Redfield came in minutes later and situated me like a regular Pap exam. After the speculum was in, Dr. Redfield said, "All right, you're going to feel some burning here. I'm applying some solution to your cervix that will help guide me to the abnormal cells. It's not the most comfortable."

"Okay," I said, trying to be brave. But then the burning started, and I dug my nails into Aaron. Surprised, he gave a little yelp before collecting himself, patting my shoulder and taking the pain.

"Almost done, Brynne. You're doing great." Again, Emmy Jo's birth scene flashed before my eyes. I leaned my head back and tried to ignore the feeling of my vagina on fire. Trying to remember that glorious day when I met my baby girl. Trying to remember –

"You might feel some pressure here, like strong menstrual cramps while I remove the cells."

Holy fucking Jesus. Tears slipped down my cheeks and Aaron looked down at me helplessly. It hurt. It hurt so bad. I would compare it to childbirth, but let's be serious – that pain is on a whole other level. But it still hurt.

"And we're done. All done. Super, Brynne. You did a great job." The speculum was out but I didn't feel like I could close my legs yet. The burning, the cramping, did not let up. I brushed the tears from my face and tried not to sob in front of my doctor.

"Can I ask what happens next?" Aaron asked, his hand still firmly latched to mine. A feeling of déjà vu washed over me.

Dr. Redfield finished washing her hands and turned to us. I didn't even bother to try to sit up. "You can resume any activities as normal, exercise, that sort of thing. I don't recommend sex for a few days and try to avoid tampons. You said the flow is lightening up considerably, correct?"

I nodded.

"So you shouldn't need to use them, but just as a precaution I wanted to mention it. Hopefully by Tuesday I will have these results back and we can find the culprit and figure out the next step."

"Thank you for your help, Dr. Redfield." Aaron shook her hand as she excused herself from the room.

"Baby? You okay?" Poor Aaron. Just like when I had contractions or after-labor pains he was timid around me, afraid to ask the wrong question, almost chastened that he wasn't feeling my pain.

I finally closed my legs and stood up, the burning still there. "Yeah, I'm okay. That was pretty painful. I wasn't expecting that."

"How about we get some ice cream and you take a nap?"

"I like that idea. I like that a lot."

We left the clinic hand in hand, out in the abnormally warm

spring day. We didn't talk about the test again until I got the phone call on Friday. The phone call that told me I had precancerous cells on my cervix.

CHAPTER 10

Portland

At the beginning of April, I almost felt like I was returning to normal. Trent hadn't gone on another business trip since his two-weeker, things had been peaceful between us, and nothing was arousing my suspicions. I went through the motions of the days – working at the store, cooking dinner, making love to my husband at night. We had our Thursday night dinners with the Roperts and the four of us continued making plans for late July to head to New York. Brynne seemed a little off, but her mood had been strange for the past few months, if I sat and really thought about it. We had a girls' night planned for Saturday: mani/pedis at the salon, followed by dinner and then a marathon of The Housewives reality show. I had been TVo'ing the episodes weekly in preparation for the event. Trent was going to be gone most of the night at a business dinner, and promised not to disturb us once he was home.

The Thursday before, we got home well past midnight from the Roperts. We had a bit of a casual night, with Brynne making spaghetti with meatballs, cheesy garlic bread, and I provided the blueberry pie. My friend seemed more distracted than usual and I think she may have actually forgotten about the dinner, the way she was rushing around once we got there and dinner being eaten a tad later than usual. I was hoping she might have said something to me once we took our wine to the deck and enjoyed the spring breeze rolling in but she remained closed-off – something else unusual for Brynne. I vowed not to let her off the hook this coming Saturday.

"Does Brynne seem okay to you?" I asked Trent as we got out of the car and walked in the house later that evening.

He flipped the kitchen lights on and placed the keys on the hook. "Yeah, why?"

"I don't know, something just seems off about her. I can't figure out what it could be."

"She didn't seem any different to me. Don't go prying into people's lives, Portland. If something is wrong and she wanted you to know, she would tell you. She's your best friend."

"I know that," I said, feeling indignant. "But also as her best friend and someone who talks to her on a daily basis, I can see that clearly something is going on. I'm confused and a little hurt that she won't talk to me about it."

Trent sighed, walking into the kitchen and reaching into the fridge for a beer. He held one out to me, but I shook my head. My three glasses of wine after dinner were more than enough. "Just let it go, Port. She'll come to you soon enough – isn't that what you always say?"

For some reason – alcohol, stress, whatever – tears filled my eyes. "I don't feel like you're listening to me, Trent, and it's hurting my feelings."

"What the hell do you mean? I'm listening and I'm giving you feedback. What more could you possibly want from me?"

I tried to figure out why I was starting a fight. Was it because I wanted to say something about the paper I found? Because I wanted him to know I was scared of our marriage being in trouble, of him being mixed up in something he shouldn't? "Maybe I want my husband to be around more, ever think of that one?"

Trent's look was one of complete surprise. "So now you have an issue with my traveling? It's always been this way. Where is this coming from?"

"I'm frustrated. Frustrated that you're always gone and you leave me here alone or you make me go to your stupid business dinners with your stupid associates and their even stupider wives. And that you put so much pressure on me to quit EJs. What the hell would I do if it weren't for my job? Sit around and get Botox all day?"

I took a deep breath, surprised by myself. While Trent knew I wasn't a fan of the other wives and quitting my job I had never, ever been so vocal about it.

Trent set his beer on the countertop, taking his time with a response. "Portland. This is my career. This is my life. My business is my life. I thought you understood that about me."

I lifted my chin defiantly as I met his gaze. "Well, I'm saying that I don't understand now. Something seems different, Trent, and I don't like it."

His eyes sharpened. "And just what do you mean by that?"

I thought quickly, trying to calm myself down and not get carried away. "The longer trips away – you're not, you don't have someone on the side, do you?" At the last minute I decided to go the cheating route. It was more easily explainable, more realistic. And maybe Trent would catch on that I knew something was up and he would stop everything on the side – if there was something to be stopped.

"What? Portland, no. Come on. You don't believe that, do you?" He was instantly by my side, wrapping me in a hug. I could feel his heart pounding through his shirt.

"I don't know what to think, Trent. You're gone for so long, so far away, going out with all these different people. And I just sit at home trying to think of ways to entertain myself. What am I supposed to think?"

"Baby, please listen to me. There is no one else. No one. I promise, I promise, I promise. I would never do that to you."

I pulled back and looked him in the eye. "You would never do something so terrible to me, would you? Or anything else?"

Was it my imagination, or did his eyes flicker for a moment? "I would never cheat on you, Portland. You're my wife and I love you. You have to believe me."

I knew my hug was still stiff when I responded, "I believe you wouldn't cheat, Trent." But I didn't believe there wasn't something else going on. He had just proved that to me. I would almost prefer cheating over drugs. Drugs killed.

✂✄

Friday I worked at EJs by myself until Serena came in after school to be on the closing shift. Trent and I stayed in that night, ordered take-out, and just watched TV. I didn't try to pry any further into the situation, and Trent was very loving and considerate of me the whole night. I did feel a little bad tricking him into thinking I suspected him of cheating, but those feelings disappeared when I thought of the drugs. I had been racking my brain to try to figure out how exactly I could get him to spill the beans, but so far I was clueless. I needed proof. I needed to get a copy of the paper I found in his office, but that was small bananas really. I wasn't sure it would be enough to get him to spill anything.

I tried to push all thoughts from my mind as I opened the front door and greeted Brynne on Saturday afternoon. "B! Long time no see," I joked, since we had only been apart since Thursday.

"P! You're still alive," she countered with, giving me a hug. "I brought wine!"

I grabbed the bottle of white from her hands and shut the door behind her. "Good, because I could use a glass right now."

We stepped into the kitchen, where I immediately brought down two wine glasses from the shelves and Brynne helped herself to the utensil cabinet and went to work opening the bottle.

"Not that I'm judging, because I could use a glass myself, but is everything good on your end?" Brynne asked as she popped the cork out.

"Oh, yeah. Just looking forward to a nice, relaxing day with my best friend."

"You guys stayed in last night?"

"We did. How about you?"

"Yep. Three lazy peas in a pod at home. And I still slept until after nine this morning."

"Whoa! Get down with your bad self," I teased, grabbing my filled glass from her. "Aaron took on EJ duties this morning?"

Brynne's eyes flicked. "Yes, he let me sleep in."

"Sounds pretty nice of him. Did you have a glass too much last night?"

Now Brynne shifted her gaze from my mine and began looking out the window over the sink. "Oh, no. I was just tired and it was his turn. That's all."

I could feel the tension in the room. Were Aaron and Brynne having problems? Was my friend having issues in her marriage too? Not them! They were the perfect couple. And Emmy Jo? What if she got caught in the middle of ––

"Port? You all right?" Brynne was looking at me strangely, and I snapped out of my Ropert demise daydream–– nightmare.

"I'm okay. Sorry, thoughts slipped away from me there. What were you saying?"

"I was just wondering if you'd talked to your dad or Darlene lately. How's their house hunting going?"

I opened the screen door and we walked out onto the deck, taking a seat on the wicker chairs. "They seem good. They found two houses they both really love. I'm thinking about going back the weekend after Easter to walk through them and check them out myself. I don't know if I'll be any real help, but it's nice they want me involved."

"Of course. That's exciting for them. I hope they find something."

"Same here. How was the store this morning?"

"Slow as usual. Did I tell you about my plans next weekend?"

I shook my head, closing my eyes as the sun finally peeked out from a cloud and warmed my face.

"We're having dinner with Juliette and Christopher Mabry. And their son, Colin. He and Emmy Jo are in the same daycare class."

"Oh, that's right. Long red hair?"

"Yep."

"You seem excited," I observed with a wry smile.

Brynne shrugged. "It's always nice to get out and do something, especially when Emmy Jo can have a play date, but I'm not sure how I feel about Juliette."

"She's kinda gossipy, right?"

"Kind of? More like that's all she wants to do. I just wonder sometimes what she says about me to the other moms."

"Oh, come on. She can't say anything that bad. What would she have to talk about?"

Again, Brynne looked uncomfortable. Again, I wondered about her and Aaron.

"Nothing, I suppose. But I always just wonder."

"Well, I hope the dinner goes well. You can always call me in for back-up if need be." I smiled at my friend, trying to cheer her up.

"Thanks. I just may take you up on that offer."

We enjoyed the warm weather as we finished our glasses, then headed back inside to get ready for the salon. We loved going in casual clothes, which was basically our workout gear. We each put on a pair of black yoga pants (for the slimming effects), and I slipped on a pink Under Armour shirt and Brynne a blue EJ Reads T-shirt. We wore flip-flops in preparation for our pedicures, and piled into the Lexus to head to town. Trent had insisted he needed the BMW for the day, and I hadn't argued.

After checking in at the salon and picking our nail colors – red for each of our toenails, a light pink for Brynne's fingernails, dark blue for mine – we settled in the pedicure chairs with a bottle of water and stack of rag mags each. Soon enough our feet were being scrubbed, massaged, and overall tickled by two young females, who spoke quietly to one another.

"This is just what I needed today. I've been so exhausted lately." Brynne sighed and leaned back in her chair. I watched her chest rise and fall as the vibrating chair worked its magic on her back.

"Everything all right with you, B?" I finally managed to ask. Maybe it was because of how relaxed I was, or that Brynne's strange attitude clearly wasn't leaving.

Her shoulders tensed, and she seemed to catch herself doing it and promptly dropped them. "Oh, P. Things are...okay. A little stressful right now."

"Do you want to talk about it?" Finally, we were getting somewhere.

"Maybe. Not right now. I just want to relax. These stones feel amazing."

"They do feel great," I agreed, as hot stones were pressed into our soles. I stayed silent for another beat, then said, "You know if you need anything I'm here for you, right? Anything, Brynne."

She leaned across the chair and patted my hand. "I know. I know."

We were quiet the rest of the pedicure, then shuffled our way to the manicure station once our toes were polished and declared perfect. I slipped my feet under the UV light and surrendered my hands to the manicurist, who got to work filing, buffing, and clipping. Even though we were right next to each other, Brynne and I were mostly quiet throughout. I wondered what she could possibly have going on, and I hoped she was wondering how she was going to tell me whatever it was tonight. I didn't want to push too much though. That wasn't how our friendship worked.

I paid for our salon visit (we took turns treating one another) and we slipped out of the salon, back into the Lexus. We were going to stop at my place first before heading out to dinner so we could change clothes.

When we got home, I was surprised to see the BMW in the driveway. "Trent? Are you home?" I called as I unlocked the door and walked in.

"I'm in my office, be right out!" I heard him yell.

"That's weird. I thought he would be gone most of the night," I said to Brynne. "You go ahead and change. I'll see what he's doing."

She nodded and walked down the hall towards the guest room. I continued down the hall until I got to Trent's office, and saw him closing his briefcase. "Hey, babe," I said, stopping in the doorway.

He turned around quickly. "Port! So sorry to intrude on your night with Brynne."

"That's okay. We're just getting ready for our dinner reservations. Are you home for the night?"

"No, I just forgot a few documents that are important for this dinner. I just stopped home to grab them quick and then I'll be gone."

"Okay." Was it my imagination working overtime again, or did he have a guilty look in his eyes? I wondered if he had taken the drug schedule. I willed my eyes not to flick to the top of his desk.

"Well, I have everything I need. I'll be off. Hope you have a nice dinner." He kissed my lips and we both moved down the hallway, where Brynne had just opened the guest bedroom door and was stepping out.

"Hi, Trent. Joining us for dinner?" she asked.

"Wish I could, Brynne," he said, stooping down to kiss her check. "I just forgot some paperwork here and I'm off again. You ladies have a wonderful evening though."

Brynne smiled at us as he gave me a hug and kiss on the cheek.

"See you tonight," I said, waving as he walked out the door. He gave a cheeky smile over his shoulder and the door closed behind him.

"Well, I'll just get changed and then we can be off. Do you like your nail color?" I asked, walking down the opposite hall and into the main bedroom. Brynne followed.

"Yeah. It's a little paler than what I had in mind, but it will do. Do you like yours?"

"Mine's a little bolder than I expected. First world problems." We cracked up at our manicure misfortune, and I disappeared into the walk-in closet to change.

We headed out once again a short time later, Brynne wearing a black pencil skirt and silk red blouse, me in a print maxi dress with colorful swirls throughout. I did Brynne's makeup as she requested, and she helped me pouf my hair just right. We loved getting dressed up on our nights out together. I think she enjoyed it more than myself since she rarely got time to herself at home to make sure her outfit matched, but I enjoyed it as well.

Dinner was fun and relaxing. We each had an Italian dish with two glasses of wine, though Brynne drank most of my second glass because I was already feeling tipsy and needed to drive us home. I could sense Brynne getting more and more nervous throughout dinner, and I had a feeling she was finally going to talk once we were back home. I might have rushed dinner just a tad because of that, but I hoped she didn't notice.

Sure enough, it was only two minutes from walking in the door when she blurted out, "I have some news."

My heart restricted. Was I ready to hear about her and Aaron separating? Should I confide in my doubts about Trent after she spilled her news? "Okay," I managed. "Let's sit down."

We walked into the living room and sat on the couch together, facing one another. Brynne looked down at her hands, tapping her fingers together.

"It's not good news, unfortunately," she said, drawing out the suspense.

"B, I'm your best friend. I've been able to tell something is up. I'm just glad you're finally talking about it."

"I'm sorry I didn't come to you sooner." Her eyes filled with tears and I reached over to embrace her, patting her back. "I'm just scared, P. Really scared."

"We just need to talk about it. Get it out in the open. It will make you feel better, I promise." I felt tears in my own eyes. Poor Brynne. It just wasn't fair.

"I mean, I know it's not life-threatening. I'm going to be fine. But it was just so scary to hear her say that."

My thoughts came to a screeching halt. "Wait, what? Brynne, you have to tell me what's going on." Was Aaron not leaving her?

"I – I have pre-cancerous cells on my cervix."

"What?" I was dumbfounded. Brynne was having health problems? That was a million times worse than what I thought. I felt like I was punched in the stomach.

"I found out a couple of weeks ago. I've been trying to process all the information and understand it before I started telling people."

"What? What do we do? What is pre-cancer? What can I do?"

I was immediately ready to dive in, to fight this ugly disease for Brynne. Of all people. Brynne.

"Port. It's going to be okay. Like I said, it's not life-threatening. I freaked out when I found out though, too. Anytime the C-word comes up I think that's a natural reaction." She took a deep breath and I clutched onto her hand. "I've been having some prolonged bleeding and intense cramps, so I made an appointment with Dr. Redfield. She did a Pap, and the results came back abnormal. She did what's called a colposcopy–– removing cells from my cervix to biopsy–– and that showed the pre-cancer cells."

"I still don't understand what pre-cancer is. So it's not cancer-cancer?"

"No, and the bad part of this is that we just have to wait and see what happens. It could be nothing. I have to get Paps every three months and each test has to come back normal for a full year until they consider me clear."

"And if it's not nothing?"

Brynne took a breath. "Then that's cancer, and then we have to think about treatment options."

The silence took over and I sat still, gripping Brynne's hand. She didn't have cancer – yet. The cancer could still come. But she was fine right now.

"I'm sorry, Port. I know this is a bit of a shock."

"A bit!" I practically shouted. "But please don't apologize. I completely understand. I hate saying this, but I actually wondered if something might be wrong with you and Aaron." I felt guilty admitting that, but it felt good to get it off my chest.

"Oh no! He's been so great through all of this. Coming to my appointments, letting me rest more. He's been fantastic."

"Good. Not that I'm surprised at all," I said, a smile finally forming on my face.

"Oh, come on. Trent would be the same way. We are two lucky gals," she said back.

I felt the smile waver. Would Trent care for me the way Aaron did for Brynne? I hated to admit – just to myself – that I wasn't sure. That was unsettling.

"Hey – when we finished the 5K and you were crying...it was because of this, wasn't it?" Brynne was naturally sensitive, but her tears as we crossed the finish line were a little unusual.

She nodded, looking down at her lap again. "It was so overwhelming to be running for something that could happen to me. It was so – I mean, really, all I can say is overwhelming."

"So this pre-cancer. Is that hereditary or something?" I asked, wanting to switch the topic.

Brynne cringed. "Actually, no. That's another bad part about this. The pre-cancer cells can be caused by HPV, a sexually transmitted infection."

My eyebrows shot to my bangs. Brynne – sweet, innocent Brynne – had an STD?

"I know what you're thinking. I thought it too. How the hell could I get an STD? But Dr. Redfield says it's different from all the nasty junk out there and it's considered an infection, not a disease. It also clears on its own in many cases. I won't ever know for sure how I got it – it could be from sex, it could not be. I also could have been carrying it for years without knowing. She said a lot of people never show symptoms."

I tried to wrap my mind around everything I was learning. "What about Aaron? What if he..." I trailed off, not sure how to ask.

"There is no test right now for men. They are typically the carrier, but never show symptoms or basically have anything wrong with them. How unfair, huh?" Brynne gave a laugh, but I could see a little of the light leave from her eyes. "I had sex in high school and college. It could have been from one of those guys. Or maybe not from sex at all, who knows? But Dr. Redfield did say that might be why I'm having troubles getting pregnant."

"You're having trouble?" This was the first time she mentioned that to me.

"We've been trying for months now with nothing. Dr. Redfield suggested we wait until –– if –– my Paps start coming back normal to start trying again."

"Brynne, why didn't you tell me? I'm sorry," I said softly. I felt terrible she was going through all of this without me. Sure she had Aaron, but sometimes you just needed a girlfriend to talk to.

"I'm sorry, too. It was all just so overwhelming. And I didn't want to worry you at all. Or just be a big complainer. We have Emmy Jo. We have a family. It's not cancer right now. Nothing is that terrible in my life."

"Still." I leaned over to give her a hug, feeling a flood of emotions. "Next time, come to me anytime. For anything. I'm so beyond serious, Brynne. I'm your best friend. That's why you have me."

She pulled away and smiled at me. "That goes for you too, you know. Anytime, anything, you come to me. Okay?"

She looked me in the eye, but I broke her gaze. "Gotcha. Now come on, let's grab another glass. Cheers to not having cancer!"

CHAPTER 11

Brynne

I felt a huge weight lift off my shoulders once I told Portland the news about my pre-cancer. I don't know what I was thinking holding that back from her. Well, that's a lie. I felt like Portland was hiding something from me. I couldn't put my finger on what it would be though. Her dad and Darlene? Trent? Everything appeared to be happy and content on her end, but it was just a feeling I had that something wasn't quite right. So I waited, but I finally had to burst. I was hoping she would talk to me that night after our salon date, but she seemed fine to keep all the focus on me. And I didn't want to push too hard. That wasn't how our friendship worked.

My parents were understandably upset when I broke the news to them, just the day after I told Portland. We went to their house for a Sunday visit, and after lunch of pulled pork sandwiches and mac 'n cheese for Emmy Jo, I let them know what was going on in my life. My mother cried, but she was always emotional. I tried to explain without going into too great of detail what HPV is and what it entails, but I tried to stress the importance that it was not a disease, not cancer, and could very well clear up on its own. Mom offered to come over whenever we needed her to baby-sit or just help around the house, and Dad pulled me into a fierce hug and said nothing could bring his baby down. I loved my parents.

Aaron was just as fabulous as I told Portland he was. He let me rest often, took on a lot of the household chores, and started work later in the mornings so he could take Emmy Jo to daycare. Sometimes I felt like such an invalid, but my condition was improving. Dr. Redfield prescribed me some medicine to help with the pain, and the bleeding had thankfully stopped. I was also taking a different birth control to help hormone control, bleeding, and cramping, which was a bit of a blow. We wanted another baby so badly, but it was definitely not in the cards for our near future. After a few weeks of being exhausted nearly twenty-four/seven I finally felt like I was getting my body and strength back again. I chose to take that as a sign that I wasn't sick, that I didn't have cancer. I had never known anybody with cancer before to ask, but I would think that if something that awful was residing in your body, you would just know. You would have a feeling, an itch at the back of your subconscious that something was wrong. I felt...okay. Not like I had cancer.

"Are you sure you're still up to having Easter here? Portland's only offered her place about a thousand times," Aaron said on the Tuesday before the holiday. We were out on the deck at sunset enjoying some quiet time together as Emmy Jo slept.

"No, I really want to," I said firmly. "We always host Easter, and I feel it would just be another reminder that some things aren't totally normal right now, and that's not at all what I want. Portland's offering to help me plenty with the cooking, but I can do it. Mom will come down on Friday too so that will help with Emmy Jo over the weekend. I really want it here."

"Okay, I won't ask again. I just want to quadruple-check." Aaron kissed my cheek and I settled back into his embrace, his strong chest on my back. We were sitting on the wooden bench on the deck, watching the stars.

We hadn't told Emmy Jo anything, as she would be too young

to understand. If – if – I was eventually diagnosed with cancer, we would handle that then. But for now, there was nothing life-threatening to scare a three year old with.

Aaron sighed, his warm breath fluttering strands of my hair. "What's on your mind?" I asked him. I could tell he had been agitated since dinner.

He sighed again before speaking. That was his way of letting me know something was bothering him and that he was going to tell me, he just needed more time to get the words out. A third sigh. I waited patiently, knowing after four years of marriage he didn't like to be provoked when trying to talk about something difficult.

"I just feel guilty sometimes, you know?" he finally got out.

"Guilty? What for?" I already knew where this was heading.

"What if you got the HPV from me? What if I'm the carrier, that I did this to you?"

I turned around so I was facing him, placing my legs across his hips so we were close. "Aaron. We've been through this before. It will be impossible for me to know where I got it from. It might not even be from sex or sexual contact. You can't beat yourself up or feel guilty for something that we will never know. That will drive you insane."

He picked up my hand and held it to his heart. "I'm scared, Brynne. I don't want to scare you or make you feel like you need to comfort me, but I'm actually really scared."

My heart hammered in my chest. My husband, my strong protector of a husband, had tears in his eyes as he said he was scared. I was scared myself, for the unknown. For the possibility of a cancer screening coming back with those dreaded results. I was trying to keep a brave face on, but it melted off as easily as non-waterproof mascara in the rain when Aaron said those words.

"I'm scared too, Aaron. I'm scared every day. I'm scared to go to the bathroom to see more blood. I'm scared a stomachache is cramps.

I'm scared to go every freaking ninety days to get my vagina poked and prodded and maybe have the cancer screen come back with beyond comprehensible results. Why does this have to happen?" I sobbed into his chest and he pulled me close, his big hands stroking my back and my hair. I could feel the tears rolling off his face and into my scalp, and we just held each other, crying in fear. Crying for unfairness. Crying for sickness in this world.

That night we made love, and it was the most emotional and unsettling sex I had ever experienced. We didn't speak, we weren't slow or gentle, yet we weren't rushed and passionate. It was just...different.

ଓ ଓ

Sunday came in the blink of an eye, and our house was soon full of love and laughter. Both Aaron and my parents were there, and Jim and Darlene had also made the trip. It felt wonderful to have a full house and see all the smiling faces, even though my mom asked me about three too many times if I needed to rest.

My body felt fine, my mind felt fine, my emotions were a little scattered, but overall I was just fine. Our guests were enjoying the warm April day by taking drinks and plates of appetizers onto to the deck, and Emmy Jo was a having a field day with all the excitement. She loved being the center of attention these days, doing a dance for her grandparents, telling stories to anyone who listened, and hamming it up for the camera when one would appear.

"B, your house looks fantastic. Please tell me you hired a cleaner so I won't feel so bad about doing so," Portland said, squeezing my elbow as I stood by the sink.

I smiled. "I didn't, I'm sorry. With the extras hours Serena picked up due to spring break I figured I could at least make the house tidy. And cleaning takes my mind off other things."

Portland nodded. "When is your next Pap?" She kept her voice lowered, knowing talk of vaginas wasn't for everyone.

"Not for another month or so. I'll be glad to get that first one out of the way, that's for sure."

She nodded once again before Trent called her name in the living room, and she whisked away.

I turned back to my thoughts and to some troubling information – gossip – I had heard the weekend prior.

Aaron, Emmy Jo, and I had a dinner date with the Mabry's – Juliette, the field trip mom from Emmy Jo's class, and her husband Christopher and their son Colin on Friday night. We went to Kraven's, a slightly more upscale restaurant that was still family-friendly enough for our children. Christopher and Aaron immediately started discussing work and the addition the Mabry's wanted to add to their home.

Juliette had leaned into me and said, "We're working on baby number two –– finally." She winked and I managed to smile back at her, feeling a pain in my heart when I thought of my condition.

"That's great news, Juliette. I hope that goes well for you."

"I think Christopher is just enjoying the trying part, but I'm really hoping to get pregnant by the summer at the latest. I wouldn't mind if it happened sooner of course, though I might look a little silly in my bikini and big bump when I take Colin to the beach!"

"I'm sure you'll be just fine," I assured her. "And you probably won't be the only one with a bump there."

"You're right. It's like something in the spring water here, isn't it? So many of us get pregnant right around then. What about you guys? Are you wanting to add a baby to the mix?"

Juliette's question was innocent, but I still felt that squeeze of pain. "Oh, maybe in a little while. Things are finally starting to settle down what with Aaron taking over for his dad and expanding and the store opening. But maybe soon." I hoped.

We had paused to put in our orders then – Colin and Emmy Jo insisting on both getting fish sticks with waffle fries shaped into smiley faces – and then Juliette started right back up again.

"You know who I did hear was pregnant – and not by her hunky husband?"

"Emmy Jo, please don't raise your voice in here. Indoor voice," I reminded my daughter when she started shouting to Colin about sharing the crayons.

"Colin, share your crayons. They're for both of you. Draw me a picture please," Juliette said, before leaning into me again. "Carolyn Brudis. Can you believe it?"

"Not really, no. She's having an affair?" Carolyn Brudis was a trim brunette in her early forties, whose husband was the sheriff in town. What man is dumb enough to have an affair with the sheriff's wife?

"Word on the street is that she is indeed. With – drum roll please."

I just stared at Juliette as she quietly drummed her fingertips on the table. I didn't buy into gossip nearly as much as she did.

"Her landscaper!" she finally finished, her red lips carving out a big smile.

"Her landscaper? Isn't he like – twenty-something?" I asked, having a tough time picturing any of this.

"Yes! Isn't it just like Desperate Housewives?" Juliette sat back in her seat, seemingly spent on that juicy bit. "I heard from Maya Daniels who heard from Karen at the pharmacy that Carolyn is pregnant and that Dick got a vasectomy years ago. Snip snip."

I shuddered at the image. "But sometimes vasectomy's can fail right? It doesn't necessarily mean she is cheating."

"No, but I also have some very reliable sources saying they heard right from Carolyn's mouth that her landscaper is also trimming another set of bushes, if you get what I'm saying."

I had sat back in my chair, wishing the dinner were over already. Juliette never failed to amaze me with all of her insider knowledge – and how easily she could give it away. I shuddered to think about her ever catching a whiff about me or my family. She was ruthless. I might have only been twenty-five, but I felt way too old for this kind of gossip. It was like being back in college – or high school! – all over again. Except this time it was marriages and kids that were involved.

Once dinner was served and as I was slicing into my smothered chicken breast, Juliette decided it was the perfect time to drop another bombshell on me. "So I didn't want to come across too nosey, but I've been dying to ask about Portland."

"Ask what about Portland?" I was still trying to decipher her first part of that sentence.

"You know, about what Trent is up to on his business trips. I hear some...things around town."

"What things?" I was truly confused as to what Juliette could be talking about. Portland hadn't mentioned anything to me about Trent's business trips, other than the fact that he was traveling more than usual lately.

Juliette's sharp eyes studied my face. "She really hasn't told you anything? You can tell me, Brynne. I know how to keep a secret."

I nearly choked on my green beans, taking a sip of iced tea before one could become permanently lodged in my throat. "Hmm, I can see that. But no, Portland hasn't mentioned a thing. Everything's great with her and Trent. He is traveling more, but his business is just expanding. It's quite exciting actually."

I could tell my words were going in one ear and right back out the other. "Okay, sure. But..." Her eyes darted to our husbands, who were laughing heartily over conversation. I longed to trade places with Aaron. "But–– I guess I'm not sure I should say."

My forehead wrinkled. "Why not?" It slipped out of my mouth

before I had time to think. She told me everything else, why keep this from me? Because it was my friend? Or because it was a rumor that she was only building upon? Or was it something...awful?

"I just don't have enough information yet, really. I just have a college roommate who lives up in Petosi who has dropped a few concerns to me lately. I know Trent's business expanded up there, so I was just putting two and two together."

"What kind of concerns?" I popped another piece of chicken in my mouth, following that with a mushroom. I was sure it was nothing.

"Well – and now I feel a bit awkward saying this actually, what with her past and all. It literally all slipped out of my mind until just this moment and I, well." Juliette was twisting her wedding ring around her finger, eyes darting around once again.

A sense of foreboding swept through me. "What past?" I asked calmly.

"You know – with her mom and the overdose," Juliette practically whispered, taking a slug of wine.

I didn't respond at first. It really didn't surprise me that others around Delany knew the story of Portland's mom, even though it wasn't exactly dinner conversation. I was sure one person found out who told another and it spiraled, especially if anyone like Juliette was at the helm. I did feel bad that it appeared people were gossiping about my friend, but I knew she would hold her head high against it. Portland wasn't brought down easily.

"So?" I asked point blank, wondering what she could possibly say. How could Trent and Portland's mom be connected?

"Well, it's just that a few drug busts have been happening around town. More than usual, more than what should be going on. People think a new dealer is in town, and the activity started right around the time Trent's gym opened."

I stared at Juliette. "And so you think Trent is running a drug business through his gym? That's – that's preposterous." A nice, big word. I liked to expand my vocabulary when upset.

Juliette stared down at her plate. "Please, Brynne, forget I even said anything. That was silly of me. I don't know what I was thinking."

She actually did look contrite, and I tried to remain calm. "I will forget that. Because that's a ridiculous notion. People can get very seriously hurt with those types of rumors out there." There was a note of finality in my voice. I was warning Juliette not to spread that type of gossip around.

She nodded, picking up her wine glass again. "So, did you see the latest daycare newsletter? Imagine that – prices going up again!"

"Brynne!" I startled when I heard my name, looking behind me. Aaron was walking towards me, his eyes inquisitive.

"Hi, sorry. What?" I shook myself out of my past conversations and tried to rejoin the present.

"I've been calling your name. Everyone's outside. Why don't you come out?" He slipped his arms around me and pulled me close. "Everything okay, sweetie?"

"Yes, it's fine. Just spaced out for a minute." I hadn't told Aaron about my conversation with Juliette. I hadn't told anyone. I thought about running to Portland immediately, but I didn't want to upset her more. It was just like what I had told Juliette – preposterous. I glanced onto the deck now, watching Trent pull Portland into his lap and kiss her full on the lips, in view of all our company. They were in love, they were happily married, and Trent would never pull a stunt like Juliette was implying. I was offended on Portland's behalf.

I picked up my glass of wine and followed Aaron outside. "Mommy! Gramps caught a butterfly. Look!" Emmy Jo held out a glass jar that indeed housed a butterfly, a beautiful magenta and gold one flapping its wings.

"It's so gorgeous," I said, putting an arm around my daughter.

"Can we keep her? I named her Flutter," Emmy Jo said, her green eyes serious.

"I don't think Flutter would be very happy if we kept her. She probably wants to get back to her mom and dad. But she can be our guest for a little while, okay? Then we'll release her and she'll be so happy."

Emmy Jo contemplated my words for a minute. "Okay. As long as I can hang out with her for a little bit. I would miss you and Daddy too if someone put me in a jar!"

And off she ran in the yard, talking to the jar the whole way. We all got a good chuckle out of that. I watched Emmy Jo for another beat and then sat on the wooden step next to Portland. Trent stood and joined Aaron at the grill and started to discuss Opening Day.

"What a day, huh?" Portland said, leaning her head on my shoulder. "I love these holidays."

"Same here," I agreed. "It makes me happy to know all my loved ones are so happy. Aren't you happy?"

Portland leaned up and peered at me. "You sure love the word happy, huh? And yes, happiness is a beautiful thing."

"A beautiful thing. You're right. It's a beautiful thing."

CHAPTER 12

Portland

The second week of June, I traveled to Springfield to check out three houses Dad and Darlene had their eye on. They had been through each several times, made a pros and cons list of each, and now wanted my opinion. Trent was out of town and I invited Brynne, though she had a few doctor appointments the weekend I planned on going and I sure didn't want her to miss them.

"Portland, you're here!" Darlene opened the door to Dad's house and enveloped me in a hug. She smelled of baking powder and some sort of flower – magnolia maybe. I hugged her back enthusiastically and stepped through the threshold, setting my suitcase by the door.

"It's great to see you, Darlene. Are you baking?" I asked, a new scent meeting my nostrils.

"I was just whipping up a batch of cookies is all, nothing fancy."

"Smells delicious," I commented, my mouth starting to water.

"I think they're just about done; let me go grab them out of the oven. Jim! Portland is here," she called out. I followed along behind her into the kitchen, where the patio door was open to the outside. Dad popped through moments later, a big straw hat on his head.

"Baby, you made it!" He came to me with open arms, then seemed to realize all the dirt that was covering his clothes and thought better of it. "I better go change. Don't want to get your nice white outfit all stained. I was just doing some yard work to help us sell the house. Realtor's advice." He winked at us before shuffling off towards the bathroom.

I took a seat at the kitchen table while Darlene opened the oven and removed a baking sheet. "I made chocolate chip with M&M's."

"That sounds delicious! And they're even better warm," I said, practically salivating now. With everything going on it seemed my appetite was disappearing, but when Trent was gone it would return. Strange what stress can do to the body.

"Do you want some milk, too?" Darlene asked, setting the baking sheet atop the stove.

"Yes please." I felt like a little kid waiting for her afternoon snack. It was strange for me to see this woman moving around the kitchen like Mom used to so many years ago. She fit in well, but I couldn't help but feel Mom's presence. I agreed wholeheartedly that a home of their own was a good idea.

I was soon hooked up with three big cookies and a large glass of milk, munching contentedly as Darlene described the houses to me. We had this morning and most of tomorrow afternoon booked up with the realtor and appointments. Tonight would be just the three of us and I was looking forward to it.

"I am huggable once again," Dad declared, strolling into the kitchen wearing clean jeans and a T-shirt. His thinning hair was wet and he smelled like body wash when he hugged me. "Great to see you, sweetie. How was your drive?"

"Not bad at all for a Friday. I think I waited long enough for any rush hour traffic to be done and over with."

"And where is Trent this weekend?"

"He's up north again. Petosi tonight and most of tomorrow. The gym has really taken off there. It's the first big gym in the area so their membership levels have been really high since the grand opening a few months ago."

"Terrific news!" Dad exclaimed, grabbing a cookie from the cooling rack. "That's what we like to hear. And how is the store doing? Brynne still liking her business venture?"

"Oh yeah, she loves it. Even though the bookstore doesn't do nearly as well as the coffee shop and café."

"I hear those eReaders are just taking over. More and more bookstores keep closing down. It's so sad," Darlene commented, walking to the table with a glass of milk for Dad.

"It really is. The big chains can't even seem to keep up. I told Brynne that everyone else is going to close down and EJs will be the only bookstore around, so maybe it's a good thing! Thank goodness for the cafe."

We all got a chuckle out of that, and Dad hopped up saying he was going to order the pizza.

"I was planning on making that delicious shrimp mac n' cheese recipe tonight but I just ran out of time to go to the store. But I'll make it for lunch tomorrow so you can have some leftovers to take home," Darlene said, patting my hand.

I finished my glass of milk, wiping my top lip. "You don't have to do that," I protested, but Darlene held up her hand to stop me.

"Don't worry, it's not just for your benefit. I can't get enough of that stuff!"

We laughed, then started chatting some more about the store and then Emmy Jo and then my upcoming trip to New York.

"Did Lucy email you the details on your lunch? I know she is so excited to meet both you and Brynne."

"Yes, I got her email. We're looking forward to it. I can't wait to meet her, and then just for a vacation in general. It'll be nice to get away for a while." It would be even nicer to get away from my husband as well, but unfortunately he was a part of the trip, of course.

"Good, I'm so tickled for you two to meet."

"Pizza's ordered!" Dad announced, coming back into the kitchen. "Port, we have a few of the pamphlets on the houses to show you. That will give you a better idea of what you'll be walking into tomorrow." He spread the papers onto the table, along with the pros and cons list of each house.

We started going through the three, and it was fun to watch how excited Darlene and Dad were for this next chapter in their lives. It reminded me of the time Trent and I were building our home. It was so exciting, so new, such an adventure. I was filled with love and contentment. Who knew that only a few short years later I would be talking to divorce lawyers behind Trent's back? That I would be the source of town gossip amongst the other ladies who talked freely about my husband possibly running a drug business? Until even last week I wouldn't have had such a thought. How things can change in the blink of an eye.

I lay in my childhood room that night on a small twin bed that had been bought when I was a freshman in high school. The tears streamed hard and fast. This house, the memories, the ghosts peeking from the corners seemed to be taunting me. I had nearly confirmed Trent was dealing drugs. I heard the whispers around Delany. I finally hacked into Trent's email and saw the written words. I printed out pages and pages to show my lawyer, to show Trent eventually. He acted like I knew nothing – and maybe he really thought that. But he wasn't going to get away with it much longer. Not only would I be granted a divorce, but his ass would be in jail. I would make sure of it.

Ϙ ϛ

Saturday morning, I awoke around eight to a text message from Trent. I could tell I hadn't been sleeping well since such a soft *ting* could wake me up. I rolled over and unplugged my cell from the charger, opening up the text.

Have a nice day with your family. Tell D & D I say hello. I love you.

I darkened my phone without responding. I could tell Trent thought something was wrong with us, because he had been almost over the top lovey dovey and attentive. Even the sext text talk had started decreasing. I was trying to act like nothing was wrong, but it was getting more difficult with each passing day. I couldn't believe the man I had married – the man I was once so in love with – could betray me in such a way.

I was in the bathroom at Emmy Jo's daycare when I heard the first rumor. Aaron was working and Brynne was at the doctor so she asked me to pick EJ up from daycare. I had arrived twenty minutes early (I was always paranoid I would be late and leave Emmy Jo stuck with a teacher) so I ran to the restroom while waiting. I was in the stall when I heard the door open and could hear voices, though I couldn't identify who they belonged to. The conversation made my stomach roll and roll and roll, but luckily I held the vomit in until they were gone.

"I almost can't believe that. Where did you hear that from?"

"I have family in Petosi. Heard it straight from them. They've been having drug busts at the schools now and bringing in drug dogs and everything."

"That poor town. And they think Trent Dolish is behind it?"

I had froze, wanting to put my feet up. I needn't have been worried though – the women were so busy gossiping they didn't even think to check if someone else was in the bathroom. And why would they think it would be me of all people in a daycare restroom? They probably didn't care if it was another mom because the rumor would eventually get to her anyway.

"The drug problem started right around the time the gym was

opened. Four employees of the gym have been caught in the busts. My sources say the police are gathering evidence against him to nail him hard. Prison time for sure. There are high school students being caught with cocaine. Cocaine. If he has any part in ruining these kids' lives he deserves everything that will come his way."

"You don't think his wife knows, do you?"

"Portland? I can't imagine. You know her mom died of a heroin overdose, don't you? I can't imagine she would take it lightly if her husband was a dealer. She's probably in the dark, like most women in marriages. It's so sad."

The woman's voice did actually sound sympathetic, which only made my stomach hurt worse. And how did everyone know about my mom? I rarely told anyone about the true reason she died; I always just said she passed away when I was younger.

It wasn't long after that conversation when the women thankfully left and I vomited into the toilet, my thoughts spinning. It was one thing for me to have my suspicions, but to hear other members of our community talk so openly about it made me lightheaded and dizzy. What the hell was Trent doing? Could he possibly be dealing drugs, letting kids younger than eighteen get their hands on them? Was I married to a monster?

"Portland, honey? You awake?" Dad's voice jolted me back to the present.

"Yep, I'm awake. Going to hit the shower soon," I answered, keeping my voice steady.

"Great. How would you like your eggs?"

"Sunny side up, please." I had to smile, thinking of all the times Dad made me his famous eggs in this house. Any time I wanted them, any way I wanted them, he would make them for me. It was nice to remember a good memory in this house.

"Those will be ready for you once you're ready." I heard his footsteps continue down the hallway and pulled the covers off me. I needed to concentrate on Dad and Darlene today. I needed to put my problems aside for at least this day. The divorce lawyer was doing all the work for me now. It was just a waiting game.

"Good morning, everyone," I said a half hour later, after a quick shower and changing into khaki shorts and a loose purple tank top. Summer was officially in Maine and the days were hot. My only complaint about the weather so far was that I hadn't been to the beach nearly enough to satisfy me.

"How did you sleep, Portland?" Darlene asked, bringing a cup of coffee to her lips and taking a sip.

"Oh, just fine, thank you. I think I'll pour myself a cup if you don't mind." I gestured to the coffee pot and Dad reached into a cabinet and grabbed a mug for me. It read Worlds #1 Dad in red letters and I recognized it from a school trip I took in the eleventh grade to Boston, where I found it at a gift shop. I smiled as he poured the steaming coffee, feeling that wave of contentment again. Dad was at the stove making eggs, Darlene reading the newspaper at the table. It felt like…family. Like home. That was such a foreign concept to me. Sometimes I could feel that way at Brynne's, like I was her sister, but it was different with family. And it made me so happy for my dad.

As I was sitting at the table reading the paper, finishing the last of my eggs, Dad excused himself to go out into the yard. Darlene and I sat in comfortable silence for a few moments, until she cleared her throat. I looked up to see her gazing gently at me. I cocked my head, wondering what she was about to say.

"How is everything at home?" she started off with. I remembered the weekend when I first met her and the concerns she voiced over Trent. What had I said to her? *Think quick!* I had talked about having a baby, how I wanted one but didn't want to be alone so often. With my story in place, I felt confident to answer.

"Everything is great, Darlene."

She nodded her head, not looking like she believed me. "And how about Trent? Sounds like he is still traveling quite a bit."

"He is, but everything is good. Still hoping to settle down in the next few years so we can start trying for those babies." I tried to set my face into a content mode, showing sympathy for my busy husband and my womanly desire to produce offspring.

Darlene gazed at me for a beat longer. She looked so wise then; I wondered for a moment what her back story was. How could she know so much about me and my life – know that there was a problem – when she barely knew me?

The conversation was over once Dad came back through the door, announcing we had to leave in fifteen minutes to make it on time to the first appointment.

After finishing my breakfast and helping to clear the table, we got into Dad's pickup truck and headed for the first home. We traveled past an expansive preserve with thick trees before seeing houses again. Dad pulled into a large white house on the left hand side of the road. I noticed the houses weren't real close to one another, and they had plenty of space and land to themselves. Dad would like that.

We met with the realtor in the driveway, a woman probably in her fifties with short blonde curly hair and a weathered tan. We shook hands and she introduced herself as Tammy, and then the tour began. We looked around the outside first. There was just over one acre, and I could tell Dad liked the wide open space and privacy. I knew living in the suburbs would never be an option for him because he did all his wood-working at home, and it could get quite loud.

We stepped inside the house, and Tammy took over. "There is exactly 1,900 square feet of living space in this Colonial home. The kitchen has newer appliances so you wouldn't need to worry about doing any upgrading."

"And they are all included?" I asked, running my hands over the sleek black refrigerator. I liked that the appliances all matched, and the black looked good with the dark stained wood of the cabinets.

"That's right, all included," Tammy confirmed. "There's hardwood floors throughout, and in here is the formal dining room."

We toured the upstairs next, where there were three bedrooms. I noticed there wasn't a bathroom in the master bedroom, and only one for the entire upstairs.

"We did think of that," Dad said when I pointed it out. "But most of the time it's just going to be the two of us, except for when we have family stay. So it might not pose such a problem as one might think."

We explored the rest of the house, including the garage and unfinished "bonus room" above that. Dad and Darlene didn't have any great ideas on what to do with that space besides possibly more storage.

After the tour, we got in the car and followed Tammy to the next location. "What did you think, Portland?" Dad asked as we wove along the streets.

"I thought it was nice. I think maybe it was too much space and too much space that will go unused," I answered honestly. "And with how big the house is compared to the bathroom space was a bit confusing. But I loved how open the yard was and all the privacy you would be afforded."

"You sound like our pros and cons list," Darlene said with a smile.

The next house reminded me of the first with the location, tucked back behind the main road and nestled more in the country. Trees and foliage surrounded the home, which from the outside looked like a cute modern ranch, nothing too big or showy. The inside was a different story.

"I can't believe how big it is!" I exclaimed when Tammy opened the door. The inside had an open floor plan, dark hardwood floors, and a beautiful chandelier in the entryway. "This is gorgeous," I continued, my head whipping every which way. "How many square feet is this?"

"Just over 2200," Tammy answered.

I looked at Dad and Darlene. "Do you need that much space?" I questioned.

"Well, let's take a look first. Here is the kitchen." Tammy showed me around, pointing out things such as the appliances that would need an upgrade and the beautiful sprawling deck that was attached off the kitchen. What I liked about the house was that it was big but it made sense, and I could see all the rooms being used. The master suite was absolutely gorgeous, nearly double the size from the first house. There were enough bedrooms for a few guest rooms and storage, but there wasn't anything like the bonus room in the first home that made us scratch our heads.

"I'll be honest – I liked that house way more than the first," I said once we were back in the car. "You would have to upgrade the kitchen and maybe a few of the bedrooms, but I think it's really nice."

I saw Dad and Darlene exchange a smile, and wondered if that was their favorite overall.

The third house was quaint, and definitely smaller than the first two. While the word cozy came to mind I wasn't sure it would be enough, especially if they entertained family and grandkids all at once. The house was filled with upgrades and was the most move-in ready out of the three, but it felt almost too modern on the inside for what I envisioned them in.

"So, you got an idea of all three. What's your favorite, little girl?" Dad asked once we were back in the car and headed home. It sunk in then how tired I was after a day of house shopping – and it wasn't even for me!

"I have to say the second is my favorite, hands down. I think the other two would work just fine for you, but I'd say the second is my choice."

Dad reached across the center console and held Darlene's hand. "That was our favorite as well."

"I guess it's been decided. I'll call Tammy tonight and we'll get our offer in right away," Darlene said, her smile beaming.

"I'm so excited for you two! A new home to call your own. What a great thing. Congrats, you crazy kids," I teased. The pain from losing my childhood home and moving on in yet another way was subsiding. I was happy, my dad was happy, and we had embraced this great new woman into our little family. If only I could get my own life straightened out.

CHAPTER 13

Brynne

"And then he pulled my hair! I had to rub my head all day and Charlotte said my hair was, was, was going to fall out!" Emmy Jo was known to stutter when she got flustered or excited, which was the case on this Wednesday night as we were eating dinner.

"Your hair won't fall out, pumpkin. I think you made it even prettier today." Aaron was quick to come to EJ's rescue, fondly patting her fine hair. She didn't seem so convinced.

"I told Miss Amber and he had to sit in the corner for pulling my hair."

"Well, let that be a lesson to you, baby. Respect other people and their bodies and then you won't have to go into a timeout yourself. Hopefully Guy learned a valuable lesson today," I said, setting my fork on the plate and leaning back in my chair.

"I'm stuffed, how about you?" Aaron asked me, also pushing away his plate of food. We made burgers on the grill that night, even though it was almost too warm to be outside. I had to slather Emmy Jo's entire body with sunscreen before allowing her outdoors.

"I couldn't eat another bite. Thank you for that delicious meal." I stood and started gathering our plates, Emmy Jo grabbing one more crinkly fry from her plate before declaring herself done as well.

"I'll do the dishes tonight. Why don't you just relax?" Aaron stood behind me at the sink and rubbed my shoulders. It felt like heaven.

"I can help out, babe. Really, I feel fine. I promise."

"How about you just stay in the kitchen then and watch me. Maybe I'll even do a little dance for you." He performed a weird hip shake ritual that was more geriatric-looking rather than Magic Mike.

Emmy Jo giggled from where she still sat at the table. "Daddy, you dance funny!"

He shrugged, an easy grin on his face. "Hey, I gave it a try. And I know you liked it." He did it again, this time bumping against my hip.

I couldn't help but laugh and give him a kiss on the lips. "I adore you, you know that? Let me get Emmy Jo cleaned up and then we'll be back. Maybe we can start making dessert for tomorrow night."

"Yay! I want to see Aunt Portland!" Emmy Jo said as I helped her down from her seat.

"She'll be here tomorrow with Uncle Trent. Will you help me make the brownies tonight?" I asked my daughter as we walked to the bathroom.

"Yes!"

I helped her get cleaned up, go to the bathroom, and wash her hands. When we returned to the kitchen, Aaron was holding my cell phone and reading the screen. "Bad news, babe," he said, holding the phone out to me. "They can't make it tomorrow."

"What?" I took the phone and glanced at the text from Portland. *Sorry B going to have to cx dinner tmrw. Talk later.*

I looked at Aaron, anger and disbelief in my eyes. "This is the third times she's cancelled plans with me. Something is not right."

Aaron glanced at Emmy Jo before responding. "I'm sure everything is fine." I knew he didn't want to get into the discussion in front of our young impressionable daughter, and I suddenly couldn't wait to put her to bed so we could have a grown-up conversation.

I was hurt, mad, confused – my emotions were all over the board. Why wouldn't Portland – my best friend of nearly a decade – talk to me?

Later that evening, I lay in bed while Aaron was in the bathroom. I propped myself up on the pillows and stared into space, still reeling from Portland's most recent cancellation. It was so unlike her. Even if Trent couldn't make it she was always game. It was our thing. Sure we were all adults and I didn't want to act like it was huge deal, but something told me there was more going on. And the rumors around town were getting harder to ignore. I was worried they would start getting around to Portland, and then I would feel terrible for not warning her. But how could I if I didn't even see her?

The bathroom door opened and Aaron appeared, a toothbrush against his teeth. "Lay it on me, babe. What's going on with our friends?"

I sighed, tucking my chin into my chest. Even Aaron knew something was clearly amiss. It had been weeks since he had seen Portland or Trent, very rare. He asked me two weeks ago if I had been hearing the latest rumors (citing a guy from work told him) and how it involved our friends, and I had to be honest. I couldn't keep hiding from it.

"I don't know what to do, Aaron. Do I confront her about what I've heard? What if she has heard people talking? What if she has just barricaded herself in their home and isn't coming out, doesn't want to face all the people talking about her? I feel so sad for her as her friend, but then I feel mad. Why isn't she talking to me? I can help her, or at least support her. What if Trent is dealing drugs? It makes me sick that she is in that house with him. What if he's doing drugs, too? There are just so many questions, no answers, and I hate the silent treatment I'm getting. Then she has the–– the audacity to keep lying to me and making these excuses. I – I feel like

I don't deserve this." The tears flirted with my lashes. Those were all my true feelings. I felt like I deserved better from my best friend. She shouldn't treat me like someone who was helping spread the rumors. If she thought I had any part in that and that was why she was ignoring me, well, that only made my heart hurt worse. I would never do something like that. I thought Portland would know that.

"Oh, honey." Aaron disappeared into the bathroom and I heard him spitting and the water running. He came out moments later and sat next to me on the bed. "I wish I knew what was going on with her. If Trent is doing something as awful as people are saying, I think Portland's health and well-being is our first concern. But I just can't see Trent being a drug dealer. He loves his wife, that is obvious. He has a good career and makes good money. Why would he throw all of that away? And you've told me the two of them have discussed having children – I can't imagine he would have a kid if he were involved in drugs. I mean, Brynne, think about it. We've know Trent for years. Do you honestly think he could be living a double life?"

I thought about it for a few moments, really thought about it. With my head on Aaron's chest, I flashed through everything I knew about Trent – he had no family now besides Portland. He was an only child and both his parents were deceased. He fell in love with Portland at first sight and never bothered to hide his love and affection for her. He treated her like a queen, he was good friends with my husband, and he was a good friend to me. He was a great uncle and godfather to Emmy Jo and she loved being around him. We took trips together. There was just no way Trent Dolish was living any sort of double life.

"There's just no way," I concluded aloud.

Aaron squeezed my shoulder. "I believe that. So now we have to make sure Portland knows we are on her side one hundred percent. When is she at the store next?"

I shrugged. "She was scheduled two days this week but asked me to fill them for her. Should I just show up at her house tomorrow and demand she talk to me?"

"I don't think that's a bad idea. I'm sure she will probably be grateful for it, honestly. Try to get her to come to dinner, maybe even just by herself. And we're going to New York in two weeks. I really can't see them backing out, as everything has been pre-paid for. We want to make sure they know we stand behind them no matter what this town makes up in their crazy minds. They're our friends."

I nodded, feeling strengthened after our talk. "You're absolutely right. I'll see if your mom can fill in at the store for a bit tomorrow so I can go over there."

Aaron stripped down to his boxers and shut out the lights. He crawled into bed and put his arm around me, drawing me close to him. "Thanks for talking to me, babe. I feel so much better," I said.

"Anytime. I got you, babe."

I laid in bed thinking long after Aaron fell asleep. What was going on with Portland, and could I get her to tell me? Over our years of friendship we had settled into a comfortable pattern. We were always there for one another but we never really went too deep into ...anything. Sometimes I questioned our friendship, but she had been by my side for so many years, how could that be? But she always seemed closed off when it came to certain things – her mom being a big factor. And now this stuff with Trent. Even though neither of us liked to talk about that kind of stuff, this was getting a little out of control. She should be able to come to me.

I always thought the reason Portland didn't come to me more was because she thought I lived in some sort of protective bubble. It was just little comments she made about my perfect life and perfect husband and perfect daughter and perfect home. I wished she would open her eyes. Life wasn't perfect – for anyone. Aaron could work extremely long hours when he was on a big project, and even when he was home it could be like his mind was still in the office. Emmy Jo was a pretty good kid, but who doesn't throw temper tantrums at the worst time (like in the grocery store?) And being a mom could be agonizing. After giving birth the world turned...scary. Going to the pool or to the beach was terrifying. What if she slipped out of my gaze and drowned? What if I turned my back for one second at the playground and someone snatched her? But I couldn't talk to Portland about those fears, because I was afraid she would just brush me off. After all, she thought I had the perfect life.

I flipped over in bed, snuggling closer to Aaron. Yes, sometimes I did question our friendship. And that was an unsettling feeling.

ও ও

The next morning, I felt on edge. I woke up Emmy Jo and went through our morning ritual, but that feeling wouldn't go away. When Aaron started to load up the vehicle to drop EJ off at daycare, I stopped him. "I'm going to walk her up today. I could use some fresh air."

"Will you be late to the store?" he asked, concern in his eyes.

I shook my head. "I'll get the Tucson packed up and jog back, then just change in the bathroom at the store. I might be cutting it close, but it'll be okay."

"If you're sure." Aaron paused for an extra beat, just looking at me. Finally, he kissed me on the lips and took off for the office.

"Want to take a walk this morning, baby girl?" I asked Emmy Jo, who was now playing with her scrambled eggs, a sign she was done eating.

"Yes! Did you put my book in my pack? Today we get special book time, Mom!"

Emmy Jo never failed to inform me of their schedule, even though we had one printed and hanging on the fridge.

"Of course. Both your dad and I put books in there for you that we think you will love, okay?" Emmy Jo nodded. "Now let's get you cleaned up and head out!"

Our walk to the school was enjoyable. The sun was peeking out, a light breeze was wafting, and Emmy Jo was alert and bouncing around, curious about everything we passed, wanting to touch everything we saw. It was moments like these with my daughter that made me reflect on life and understand everything I had. I may have been dealt a minor health issue and my best friend might be pulling away, but this was why life was worth living. Seeing the world through Emmy Jo's eyes was a blessing.

After I dropped EJ off, waving good-bye as she was led away by Amber, I nearly sprinted back to the house. It felt good to run, to stretch my legs, to breathe the crisp air and just let my thoughts fall away for a moment. I made it home in enough time that I didn't have to rush, so I took my time changing and poured myself a cup of coffee before heading out to EJs.

Once I was in the store though, the antsy feeling came back. I paced the aisles of EJ Reads and meticulously straightened books, vacuumed the floors repeatedly, and dropped a cup of hot coffee on the newly polished café floor due to being distracted. By the time Aaron's mom showed up I was practically ready to commit myself. I flew out the doors with barely a peck on her cheek, something I felt guilty for moments later as I pulled the Tucson out of the lot and headed towards Portland's home. I would have to apologize when I saw her again.

Pulling into the driveway, I gave myself a mental pep talk. *This is your best friend. She wants your help, she just doesn't know how to ask. Stop being a sissy.*

I opened the car door and cautiously walked to the front door. Ringing the bell, I stood on my heels as I waited. My ballet flats didn't provide much support, and I nearly toppled backwards when the door opened.

"Brynne! What are you doing here?" Portland looked shocked to see me. She wore workout gear – short white shorts and a neon orange running T-shirt. Her blonde hair was in a messy ponytail and she wasn't wearing any makeup. I was relieved that she looked like...Portland.

"Can I come in?" I asked.

"Yeah, of course. Come on in." She opened the screen door and I stepped inside. I tried to casually glance around. Everything seemed in place. The wall of photos I had helped Portland create after they moved in was up and all the pictures were there, including those of her and Trent and plenty of their wedding photos.

"I'm sorry I had to cancel on dinner tonight. I – something's just come up. Trent is out of town anyway so it just would have been me."

"Port, you come to dinners all the time by yourself. We love having you." I was chickening out with what I really wanted to say, which was *what the hell is going on?*

"Can I get you something to drink? Water, coffee, juice? Wine?" She deflected my statement and walked into the kitchen. I trailed behind, determined to work up the courage. I wasn't one for confrontation, and rarely had to go that route with Portland.

"Some water would be great, thanks. What are you doing tonight?"

Portland took a moment before answering, grabbing a glass from the cabinet and filling it first with ice then water from the fridge. "I, er, told Dad and Darlene I would Skype with them tonight. It's one of the last nights in that home."

"Why wouldn't you just say that? And we could have done it at my house. I would love to see them again." She wasn't telling the truth, that was obvious to me. It hurt even worse that she was now lying to my face.

Portland sighed and handed me my glass. Her eyes wouldn't meet mine.

"Portland. Please tell me what the hell is going on." There. I'd said it. Finally.

She didn't say anything, just started to examine her cuticles. I spoke again. "I know something is wrong. I'm not stupid, and I feel very offended at how you are treating me. I'm your best friend. I can tell when something is wrong. I don't like that you've been avoiding me. I want to help you."

"I'm so sorry you feel so hurt and offended, Brynne. I'm sorry your perfect life has a little chip in it all because of me." Portland's tone was sarcastic, and my head whipped back as if I'd been slapped.

"What? That's not what I'm saying at all. I'm——"

"That's what you just said, is it not? Some people have real problems. We can't all be Brynne Ropert."

This was not the way I expected our conversation to go. "Portland, did I do something? Is that why you're so mad at me? I'm really sorry, but I'm totally confused right now."

Portland took a seat on the bar stool next to me. "No. I'm sorry, Brynne. I'm under a lot of stress right now and I'm taking it out on the wrong person. This is why I've been avoiding you in the first place. I knew I would be snappy and mean and I didn't want to put you through that." She suddenly burst into tears, and all my anger faded away. It was forgotten.

I stood and put my arms around her, feeling her small body heave giant sobs. I was terrified. Something seemed to be torturing my friend. "P, please talk to me. I'm begging you. I'm scared."

It took a few minutes before her sobs calmed down. "Have you heard the town talk?"

"I have. Port, I want you to know that I wanted to tell you about what was going on. But right when I heard about it you stopped talking to me and coming around, and I didn't want to put that in a text or anything."

Portland held up her hand to stop my rambling. "I know, I know. I'm not saying you have anything to do with it or were hiding it from me. I was just wondering if you had heard."

I sat down again, holding onto her hand. "I have. The women in this town are horrible. Cruel. To make up such shoddy rumors about someone that could potentially ruin lives is just despicable. They make me sick."

Portland wiped her tears away and I jumped up, rushing to the bathroom to grab a box of tissues. I came back and handed her a few, keeping one for myself. "Is that why you haven't been going out?"

She nodded, blowing her nose. "It's so embarrassing. I don't want to be at EJs because what if one of them walks in and says something to me? I feel like I'm the laughingstock of the town right now. And everyone is talking about my mom. I swear that story seems more fascinating than anything to them."

My heart cracked a little when she said this. Portland was so closed off when it came to her mom's death. I still wondered who had found out and why people kept the talk going. Was there nothing more interesting happening?

"Have you been able to talk to Trent about this? What does he say?"

"He just tells me to grow a thicker skin. He says it will all die down soon enough and people will move on to the next thing. But it still stings. I feel like it will never stop."

"Does he know why he is being targeted?"

"Just because of some drug busts that are happening in towns where his gyms are. But they're practically all over this area of Maine now, it's not like he can help that he is successful. It's so unfair."

"Well, he has us supporting him. And you. Who cares about these stupid people in this town? I know they'll get what's coming to them. Karma is a bitch, we know that."

Portland showed a glimpse of a smile. "So you and Aaron believe that he's not involved?"

"Of course we don't! It's horrible and shocking to hear and I'll be honest with you – just last night we sat down and really talked about it. But, Port, we would know if he was doing anything wrong on the side. Trent is one of our best friends. There is no way he would do this to you, his company, or himself. He's too smart for that. And he loves his wife way too much."

I thought my words would make her feel better, but Portland tucked her chin to her chest and started sobbing again. It took me a moment to jump back in and make soothing noises, stroking her arm. "Come on, P, everything is going to be okay. Everything is going to be okay."

We sat in relative silence for probably twenty minutes, Portland's head on my shoulder and my arms wrapped around her. It was awkward and uncomfortable for me, but Portland seemed content. Her cries quieted down and soon she was barely sniffling.

"I'm really sorry I said those things earlier, B. That was so unfair of me. You know I didn't mean it, right?" Her blue eyes still shone with tears as she looked at me.

"I know. It's no worries at all. Don't think about it again. And please, come over tonight for dinner. Emmy Jo made you brownies."

A real smile finally emerged. "Mmm, brownies. With the cream cheese swirled throughout?"

"With the cream cheese swirled throughout. Aaron wants to see you, too. We've missed you, P."

"I've missed you, too. I'm sorry I just withdrew. I didn't know how to handle it. Anything. I was confused and hurting and lost and––"

"And you should never go through that alone. Not with me as your best friend. Now come on." I pulled her up from her chair.

"What are we doing?"

"We're going out for brunch. I'm dying for some pancakes and you could use a mimosa. On me."

"But――"

"No buts. You can't hide from this town forever, that will only make people talk more. We're going to get some grub and talk more about this trip in two weeks. If our suitcases aren't coordinated there will be hell to pay in New York."

"I almost forgot about our trip! I need to go shopping still."

"Lucky for you, I have the afternoon off."

CHAPTER 14

Portland

I lay in the guest bed at the Ropert's home on Thursday night, guilt invading my body. I hadn't meant to lie to Brynne or keep anything from her, but I just knew she wouldn't understand. It would come as a shock to learn about Trent and the divorce lawyer, and I just needed more time to understand internally what was happening to my life. My husband and I were in the process of divorcing and he was looking at prison time for multiple drug charges – and he had no idea either was coming.

I felt bad for lashing out at Brynne but my words – in all honesty – weren't untrue. I didn't think she would understand. Especially after she defended Trent and said she and Aaron knew there was no way he was doing what he actually was doing. She wouldn't get it, and she might not believe it. I understood that in a second. It hurt me to keep it from her and I knew she might be mad when she found out the truth, but it was something I had to hold inside for right now. Until I was stronger to face it head on.

While Brynne was my best friend and we had been through rough times together, her life was sparkling compared to mine. And I knew so many people have it worse than me, I got that. But if you put me and Brynne side by side, there was clearly a winner and a loser. Brynne grew up with both parents who loved her and was never afraid to let her know, help her out, and be a parent in general. The worst part of her childhood was when she almost drowned in the ocean and her father leapt in after her, pulled her to safety, and performed CPR on her until she choked up the water. I found my mother dead from a heroin overdose and then got left in the dust while my father worked through the nightmare.

Brynne went to college, met her soulmate, got married, and had a wonderful daughter. Aaron treated her like a goddess, Emmy Jo was incredible, and she even got along splendidly with her in-laws. I struggled in school, chickened out and followed my friend around while she started her new life, and married a drug dealer. Sure he wasn't one (I was nearly 100% positive) when we married, but a few short years later he was betraying me.

Brynne couldn't even get cancer. That sounded so awful and I would never ever wish cancer on my beautiful friend, but even when cancer tried to attack her body it gave her a nice warning. Who has that happen to them? Only Brynne, I tell you. If I were to get cancer, I wouldn't suspect it until I only had six months to live.

Our lives were just too different. I had tried for so many years to let Brynne in and see a life that was different from hers, but I just didn't think she could get it. And that wasn't her fault. In any way. She couldn't help it that she had a fairy godmother watching out for her and I didn't. I was happy for her. She deserved a great life because she was a great person. But just once in a while, I wish she could understand me better. I wish the veil that she sometimes wore would be slipped off and she could see the world for all the harshness and unfairness that could come with it.

And that's why I couldn't always be so honest with her. It killed me keeping it all inside. But as much as I wished that veil of sunshine and rainbows would be lifted, I didn't want to be the person that did it. I wanted Brynne to think we both led amazing lives. I wanted her to think that Trent was a great person, a great husband, and that I was filled with happiness. I didn't want her to worry about me. Did that make me a bad friend? I couldn't decide. I honestly couldn't decide. Maybe one day I'd get to be this honest with her. But maybe I wouldn't.

ಶಿ

"NYC, here we come!" Brynne was hanging out the car window on the passenger side of the Tucson as it pulled into the driveway on Friday morning.

I laughed, approaching the car with my oversized suitcase. "Someone's had what – three cups of coffee this morning?" I asked, watching as Brynne opened the door and hopped out.

She threw her arms around me in greeting. "How did you know? I'm wired and ready to go! The shops are calling our names. Can you hear it?" She got quiet and palmed one hand around her ear.

I mimicked her move. "Just the ocean," I whispered, and we burst into giggles.

"Is Trent ready to go?" Brynne asked, just as the front door opened and my husband appeared.

"Did somebody say my name?" he asked, hauling out more luggage (most of it still mine) with him.

"Hey, man. Ready for the weekend?" Aaron asked, also exiting the vehicle.

"You bet! I was giving Port hell for all the shopping she did, but I might have gone overboard on the Sox gear." He dropped his voice to a whisper for those last words, though we all still heard him.

I laughed and gave my elbow to Trent's stomach. "I still think I out-spent you, darling. Not to worry!"

Trent grabbed me and dipped me in a kiss. I tried my hardest not to tense up, to remind myself that I was a happy wife – at least that was my act. We straightened and I made sure Brynne saw my smile. She was smiling herself and I saw her exchange a look – of relief? – with Aaron. I felt a new sense of determination to get through this weekend pleasantly and not arouse their suspicions any longer. Trent and I already agreed we wouldn't mention the drug rumor; we didn't want to spoil our vacation at all.

We climbed in the vehicle, Brynne hopping in the back with me so we could chatter along the way. We were soon on I-95 heading south for the five hour drive. We stopped once for lunch in Worcester, Massachusetts, where Aaron delivered his big news.

"I got six stores on the Grand Avenue strip," he announced proudly, right after the appetizers were served.

"Aaron, that's amazing! Congratulations," I said, genuinely happy for my friends.

"Way to go, man. Six stores is a big deal," Trent said, popping a shrimp popper in his mouth.

"Thanks, we just got the news this morning. It means a lot of busy times ahead, but the project won't actually start for a few months, so I have some time to get more guys hired on to handle the workload."

Brynne squeezed Aaron's hand. "This trip is like a celebratory one now, too. I'm so proud of you, honey."

Aaron leaned over and kissed her cheek. "Thanks, babe."

I smiled and looked down at the napkin in my lap. I would not be jealous. Friends don't get jealousy issues like this.

"And how's your work, Trent?" Aaron asked, grabbing a shrimp for himself.

"Busy as ever. Hoping to expand maybe to the eastern region of the state. We haven't gotten over there much yet, so that's a goal."

"That sounds like it would be a big deal." Brynne smiled at us and I nodded back, trying to look calm and happy.

Trent leaned over and kissed my cheek, mirroring Aaron from moments before. "Good thing I have Portland holding down the fort at home. I couldn't do it without her."

I hated that I had to wonder if it was a sincere compliment, or a back-handed way of him saying he wanted me to quit work.

ॐ

After lunch we drove straight through to New York, or more specifically, Manhattan. We were staying at Hotel Wales on Madison Avenue, a short jaunt from the stadium. The inside was sleek and modern, a lot of white but beautiful dark granite throughout broke up the coloring. Our rooms were on the same floor and just across from one another. They were identical – a king-sized bed with a plush comforter and plenty of pillows, two large picture windows showcasing stunning views of the city, and a large bathroom with a whirlpool tub I couldn't wait to sink into.

"What's first on our agenda?" Trent asked as we started unpacking. I carefully hung my nice dresses and silk shirts in the closet, not wanting them to wrinkle.

"Dinner at Paola's." I named the upscale Italian restaurant that was in the same building as our accommodations. "In the morning Brynne and I are going to take a walk through Central Park. What time do we want to take off for the stadium?"

"No later than ten. The game starts at 1:05 and gates open around eleven."

"Got it. We planned on going early so we can make it back by then."

I went into the bathroom and started setting out my makeup and face products. Cleanser, moisturizer, tweezers, lotion, a comb. I scoped out the hair dryer that was attached to the wall and was pleased to find it in good condition. The shampoos and soaps left for us were high quality, though they should be for the rates charged. I didn't need to stay at such a fancy hotel, but Trent insisted. I knew Brynne and Aaron wouldn't blink an eye at the cost but it made me feel spoiled – in a bad way. I knew Trent could sense my discomfort over the weeks, but he didn't have to buy me off.

Speaking of Trent, my husband slipped his arms around me then, his hands going right to my breasts. "We have some alone time before our reservations." He nipped at my neck, but I turned around and squashed those plans.

"I have plenty of unpacking to do and then I have to get ready. You can't expect me to eat at Paola's in this wrinkled outfit." I gestured to my black capri pants and white tank top, both which had indeed become wrinkled in the car ride.

"Oh, come on, we can make it quick. I feel like I'm a virgin again so give me thirty seconds."

"Let's not be so dramatic, Trent. It hasn't been that long. And maybe it wouldn't be so long if you would actually be home for once."

Trent sighed, dropping his head in his hands. "Not this again. Port, why are you acting this way? You know I'm trying to make a good life for us. Why do you have to be so hard on me?"

My blood boiled. Making a good life for us by destroying it? Right. "I just wish you were home more. Work isn't everything. You can have a wife and a good life. You don't have to be...obsessed with your job anymore."

I looked at him, my blue eyes pleading. *Please tell me what's going on. Please tell me you aren't doing what I know you are doing. Please be my husband again.*

He just sighed and turned his back to me. "Guess it's just you and me again," he said to his right hand, making my insides squirm.

"You're so charming. I can't figure out why I'm not just jumping into bed with you," I said sarcastically, grabbing a cobalt blue dress with a lace back from the closet. "Real fucking charming."

I slammed the door and struggled to keep my emotions in check while I changed. I bent over and brushed out my hair, adding a powder to help give it some volume. I applied my makeup carefully and with precision, willing my hands not shake when I got to my eyeliner. I swiped on deodorant and spritzed myself with Chanel, another recent gift from Trent.

Feeling slightly calmer, I opened the door to find Brynne and Aaron in the room, both dressed and ready for dinner.

"You look gorgeous. That blue does amazing things with your eyes," Brynne complimented.

"You look great yourself. That's the dress you just bought a couple weeks ago, right?"

Brynne smoothed her hands down the black and white structured dress with cutouts near the top. Very fashionforward and a little un-Brynne like, but she looked beautiful. "That's right. You still think it looks okay?"

I nodded my head as Aaron said, "Ravishing, Mrs. Ropert. Simply ravishing," making her giggle.

"Well, I'll just get changed and then we can head." Trent brushed past me, kissing me on the temple before disappearing into the bathroom. I forced another smile at him for the sake of our company.

Our dinner was perfectly pleasant. I had the *linguine alle vongole*, or pasta with clams in a white wine and garlic sauce. I limited myself to two glasses of wine since Brynne and I planned on being up early and doing some exploring before the game. I did enjoy a slice of *torta di ricotta*, a delicious cherry cheesecake that we ordered for the table. We laughed and told stories; I even felt comfortable holding Trent's hand. The wine, good food, and great company of friends helped put me at ease. I even tried to brush off the "that's my girl" comment from

Trent he made after I could explain the new piece of equipment his gyms were pushing to Brynne and Aaron.

My husband could apparently sense my guard was down, because he offered me a back rub once back in the room, and before I could stop it, we were making love. I didn't hate it. I just tried to push all thoughts of drugs and divorce from my wine-addled mind.

ॐ

The next day passed in a flash. Brynne and I strolled through Central Park and chatted about our day, the game, and our plans for Sunday, which included shopping, lunch with Darlene's daughter Lucy, and more shopping. We went to the game with our husbands, which I couldn't tell you a thing about. I didn't understand the innings and the outs, I just knew that baseball took an immensely long time to watch, my shoulders got burnt from being out in the sun for so long, and that Trent and Aaron were extremely pleased that the Sox won. I ate a hot dog much to Brynne's chagrin, drank a few beers (to my own chagrin), and even participated in the wave at one point.

After hitting up plenty of bars after the game and feeling like I did back in my college days, we poured ourselves back to the hotel. There was not a chance for sex that night, as we were both too exhausted and more than a bit drunk to make it happen.

The next morning, I was a bundle of nerves. I didn't know why I was so nervous to meet Lucy. I wanted her to like me, I wanted to like her. But it would be okay if we didn't get along. It was just weird to think that in a way, I was finally getting a sister. At almost twenty-six years old. If Dad and Darlene remarried, of course. But I really didn't doubt that would happen.

"Are you getting excited?" Brynne asked me as we exited

Bloomingdale's, our arms laden down with shopping bags. It was nearing ten o'clock, and we had just enough time to hit up Barney's before meeting Lucy for lunch.

"I am. I hope we get along. I know Darlene would be heartbroken if we didn't."

"Well, you said from her emails she seems like a nice woman. And Darlene is so sweet, it's hard to picture her with a daughter who is evil. I'm sure it will all go well."

"Thanks for coming along with me. I think it will be a lot easier with your support."

"What are friends for? Now come on, we're on a time limit!" She pulled me into Barneys and we spent the next hour and a half trolling the aisles, trying on clothes and jewelry, and ultimately spending way too much on our already weary credit cards.

Just minutes before noon, our taxi dropped us on the corner of 3rd and 73rd on the Upper East Side, at a place called EJ's Luncheonette. Can you guess who picked the location? Brynne was adamant about eating at the place that shared her daughter's name, but Lucy backed up her choice saying you could get breakfast all day at the cozy diner and it was a favorite of hers.

We walked under the green awning and Brynne pulled open the door. Lucy and I had befriended one another on Facebook, so I knew I was looking for a petite blonde with eyes identical to Darlene. It didn't take me long to spot her, her eyes growing wide as we connected. A smile spread across her face and she immediately rushed up to us, opening her arms for a hug.

"Portland, it's so great to finally meet you! And hi, you must be Brynne. I've heard so much about you!" Lucy hugged Brynne next, and my friend caught my eye over Lucy's shoulder and grinned.

"It's great to meet you too, Lucy. Thank you for meeting with us," I said, giving my possible future step sister a quick once over.

According to her Facebook profile she was twenty-nine, and she wore a tailored suit with basic black pants, along with a bright pink jacket that fit her to a T. She accessorized with a chunky silver necklace, multiple bangle bracelets, and large diamond earrings. She looked fashionable yet business-like.

"My pleasure. I work just up the street so I frequent this place. I understand your daughter is Emmy Jo?" Lucy asked Brynne, who lit up at Emmy Jo's name.

"Yes, and she was just tickled when I told her where we would be eating. We call her EJ quite a bit, and I even run a bookstore and café called EJ Reads. Portland helps me out with the store."

"You'll have to tell me all about it! Let's order and take a seat. You can have breakfast, or else the salads here are amazing."

All three of us indeed ordered salads. I was trying to make up for the heavy pasta I had Friday night, combined with the ballpark food from yesterday. I had the Cobb, Lucy ordered the Greek, and Brynne had to try the EJ's chopped salad.

We got a table in a back corner, where it was a little quieter from all the hustle and bustle.

"During the week this place gets packed at lunchtime. Weekends are still busy, but nothing compared to a weekday." We set our purses on the chairs and relieved our tired arms from the shopping bags as Lucy continued to prattle on about EJs and asked us about our shopping. We would be going back to Madison Avenue to hit up some more shops on the way back to the hotel, and she gave us a few recommendations.

"What are the men doing today?" Lucy asked.

"Probably sleeping off hangovers. They got a bit rowdy at the game yesterday," I answered, a smile on my face. "But they mentioned maybe hitting up a few of the museums. I don't think they wanted to travel real far or dare take the noisy subway anywhere today."

Our food was delivered a short time later, and our talk moved to Dad and Darlene.

"Your mom is the best, Lucy. I'm so happy for Dad that they found each other. He's more alive since they've been together. I truly couldn't ask for a better partner for him."

Lucy laid her hand over mine and looked me right in the eyes. "Thank you so much for saying that, Portland. It really means a lot to me. Mom has been through a lot, and all of us kids worried about her for so many years. Not that we'll ever stop, but it's amazing that there is someone else who now cares for her so much, wants to protect her like we did all those years. I can't wait to come up for a visit and see their new house."

"You will love it." I paused for a moment, thinking over Lucy's last words. "Can I ask you a personal question?"

"Sure." Lucy shoved a forkful of lettuce in her mouth, looking at me with an open expression.

"What do you mean protect your mom? Because she got divorced?" I realized with a start I didn't know Darlene's past. I assumed she was divorced of course, though I didn't know why. She could have even been widowed, like my father.

Lucy sat back in her chair, wiping her mouth with a napkin. "Our father," she started, then paused and sighed. Brynne set her fork down, seeming to realize we were in for a story. "Our father wasn't a very good man. He was a cheater, an abuser, an alcoholic. To this day, I honestly can't figure out why Mom stayed with him for so long. He would disappear for days at a time with whatever young girl he could find, he ran them into the ground with debts, all he did was drink beer – for breakfast, lunch and supper – and he even hit Mom. It was awful." She looked down at her hands in her lap.

"I'm so sorry, Lucy. I didn't know any of that. Dad never made a mention to me." I felt terrible for asking, for Lucy, for Darlene. What a horrible thing to go through.

"Yeah, but Mom loves us something fierce, and the first time Dane laid a hand on me she was done. She called the police and showed them documented proof of all the times he had hit her. She had been slowly building up a case against him. All the times I thought she was just playing dead, she had been smart. She was taking pictures of her bruises, writing down times and dates he hit her, days he was gone, debts he had gotten us into. She had pictures of him passed out surrounded by beer cans. She had saved up enough money that we could start fresh again after he was arrested the night he hit me." She touched the left side of her face briefly, as if being transported back to that moment. "And that's when I knew my mom was a special woman. I felt bad for ever not believing in her. She knew exactly what she was doing, and she was smart about it. And now me and my brothers know we will also do anything we can to protect her like she did for us. She's a great mom."

Brynne sniffled next to me and wiped a tear from her eye. "Wow, Lucy. I didn't know any of that about Darlene, and you would never know it from talking to her. She's always so happy, so upbeat and carefree. I would never have guessed her past was like that."

"I think it's because she met your dad." Lucy smiled at me. "Mom was in a bad place for a lot of years. She felt terrible that Dane ever laid a hand on me. I always tell her it's not her fault he was a piece of shit, and that she would never allow that to happen again. That's what's important. But once she met Jim, it was like everything changed. She's happy again. She's back to being herself before Dane sucked the life out of her."

We sat in silence for a few moments. Brynne and Lucy tucked back into their lunches, but I was unable to. Darlene was a smart woman. She was being patient making her move. It spooked me, but Darlene and I had a lot in common at that moment.

CHAPTER 15

Brynne

I was hoping our trip to New York would rejuvenate Portland, bring her back to her old self. The Portland I knew and loved. But while from the outside she seemed just fine, I could tell she was still hiding within herself. Did she not know I could see her jaw clench when Trent touched her? That I could see her blue eyes fade when he kissed her? I wasn't stupid, and I was getting tired of being treated like I was.

Over the next couple of months, something happened that I never thought would – Portland and I started to drift away. She worked less at the store, cancelled Thursday night dinner multiple times, and simply stopped coming around so much. I'll admit it – the way she was treating me didn't make me want to work hard for our friendship. Did she care so little about me, think so little of me, that she couldn't talk to me anymore about her marriage being in trouble? And if so, then fine. I would focus on myself, my health, my career, and my family.

"Mommy, you look sad." I was sitting on the couch on a Thursday night, yet another night Portland had cancelled. Aaron was cleaning up the kitchen after dinner, and I was nursing a glass of wine while trying to get some reading done on the couch. Even though I was enjoying the mystery novel open in my lap my mind couldn't stay focused on the characters, much less figure out the murderer. I tried once again to focus on the words when I heard my daughter's voice. I hadn't even noticed Emmy Jo toddling into the room to join me.

"I'm not sad, baby. Mommy's just a little sleepy right now," I lied to my daughter. How could a three year old sense emotions like that? I snapped the book shut and focused my attention on her.

"Can we go to the beach tomorrow?" She switched focus quickly, making me relieved. I'd much rather talk about the beach.

"We can go. It might be one of the last times for the year, so let's make it a good trip, okay?" I said, and she nodded her head enthusiastically.

"I'll wear my green suit and build two–– no three–– sandcastles. Daddy will, will, will you help me build them?"

Aaron entered the living room and sat so Emmy Jo was between us. "You know there is nothing else I would rather do. Three sandcastles, coming right up!"

"Not now, silly! Tomorrow!" Emmy Jo cracked up, causing Aaron and I to laugh.

After we put her to sleep we came together again in the bedroom, standing at our his-and-hers vanities. I spread toothpaste onto my toothbrush and started brushing, getting lost in my thoughts. Normally I would invite Portland along to a beach day, but I just didn't want to. I didn't want to be rejected, I didn't want to hear another petty excuse. But I felt guilty if I didn't try. I picked up my phone but then set it down. Picked it up, set it down.

"What're you doing, babe?" Aaron asked, observing me.

I sighed, spitting into the sink. "Trying to decide if I should invite Portland tomorrow."

He didn't say anything, just kept looking at me.

"I feel like I should, but how many times can a person get rejected before your ego gets too crushed? I feel like she doesn't even want to be friends with me anymore. Why is this happening?" I put the toothbrush back in my mouth and brushed, feeling the bristles connect with gums.

"I don't know, honey. I'm as baffled by the Dolishs' as you are right now. Do you want me to text her and see if she'll come?"

I spit again and rinsed out my mouth. "No, but thanks for the offer. I think I'll just leave it. Whenever she wants to come around again she can. I've made all the effort I can. I don't know what to do anymore."

⚥

The next week Monday, I was back in Dr. Redfield's office for my second Pap test since my abnormal results. The first test had come back fine, to everyone's relief. But now we would have to go through the waiting game again, which was always hard.

"How have you been feeling, Brynne?" Dr. Redfield asked when she entered the room, snapping on rubber gloves and taking a seat on her stool.

I knew the drill now, and slid down the table and propped my feet in the stirrups. "I think I'm okay, really. No more bleeding or cramps, my periods have been normal each month, I don't feel sick or nauseous."

"All good news. This will be real quick."

I felt the pressure of the speculum being inserted, and just a minute later it was out. I breathed a sigh of relief and closed my knees.

"We should have the results in three days or so, and I'll give you a call when they come in," Dr. Redfield said, standing and walking to the sink.

"Thank you. Can I ask a question?"

"Of course."

"Aaron and I, we–– we would like to try for another baby. Well, we had been before all of this, like I had mentioned to you. Do you think that after all this is over – and hopefully all the tests in the year come back fine – we can start trying again?"

"I do. The cells that were in your body could have been making getting pregnant difficult, but you must see the bright side of things. It's a good thing your body was rejecting a baby, because to be carrying a child while in this situation is not healthy. Worst case scenario of course is cancer, and you would have to choose between keeping a baby and going through treatment. I think you are a lucky one, Brynne. Wait until these tests all come back normal," she patted my shoulder reassuringly, "and then give it another go."

I left the doctor's office that day feeling better than I had in a long time. It's funny the way the world works – hell, it's funny the way the human body works. I couldn't imagine choosing between keeping my baby and getting cancer treatment. I had dodged an incredibly tough situation, but I couldn't wait to begin trying again for another baby. If all the tests were clear.

ᛒᛯ

Monday afternoon I was sitting behind the counter at EJ Reads, adding more pictures to the scrapbook for Emmy Jo. I carefully glued down a picture of her and Portland, taken at the beach in the early summer, when Portland was still a major part of our lives.

I swiped a tear that appeared, feeling again the pang inside. Was our friendship over? Just like that? How could Portland walk away from seven years of friendship? Why? I shook my head and grabbed another photo from the stack, this one of Emmy Jo with Aaron's parents. My spirits lifted. Family is what we are all left with in the end. I had heard that saying before, but I always considered Portland a part of the family, not just a friend.

I heard the front door creak open and looked up from my project. "Port." I was shocked to see my friend standing in the doorway, walking hesitantly my way. "You're here."

"I'm here. And I'm sorry, B." She burst into tears and I jumped up, rushing over to her and wrapping my arms around her. Her full weight sagged against me and I couldn't hold us both up. We fell to the floor in a heap, Portland not letting go.

We stayed on the floor for at least fifteen minutes, both crying. While I didn't know why she was crying, I knew why I was. My friend was hurting. That hurt me. Something was seriously wrong with Portland.

"Do you want to come back to the house? Serena will be here in about fifteen minutes. We can talk. How does that sound?" I stroked her blonde hair and wiped her cheeks with my sleeve.

She nodded, and looked up at me with soulful blue eyes. "I'm scared, Brynne."

My heart felt cracked in two. What was she scared of? Trent? Rumors? Something worse?

I helped Portland outside and into my vehicle, not wanting her to drive anywhere. I rushed back into the store and grabbed my purse from under the desk, watching the clock until it hit three and Serena walked in, right on time. I gave her rushed updates and then was out, the door slamming shut behind me as I made a hasty exit.

Portland and I didn't talk on the way home. I concentrated on getting there in one piece, and Portland heaved big sighs in the passenger seat, clutching the bottom of her T-shirt. I pulled in the driveway, thankful Aaron was in the office all day and would pick up Emmy Jo from daycare. I had planned on staying at the store most of the night to work inventory, but all those thoughts had clearly evaporated.

We exited the Tucson and walked into the house, my arm

around Portland. I worried if I didn't prop her up she would collapse again. I opened the door and led her straight onto the couch, then zoomed off to the kitchen to get her a glass of water and grab a box of Kleenex.

Settling on the couch next to her, I put the box between us and handed her the glass. I didn't say anything. I just waited.

After what seemed to be an eternity but was probably only five minutes, Portland took a deep breath and let it out. "Trent and I are getting a divorce."

"What?" I all but shouted. I was shocked. A divorce? Portland and Trent were the happiest couple I knew. Sure the rumors were probably a strain, but couples worked through problems. That was a marriage. I bit my lip, not wanting to verbalize those thoughts. That probably wouldn't help the situation any.

"Things have become…difficult," Portland stated, not meeting my eyes. "Trent's become like a different person since all the rumors started. And he keeps just disappearing. He's running away from all the problems and it's not helping us figure anything out or move on or put on a united front. He runs and I'm stuck here to deal with everything. We keep fighting about it and – and I just can't take it anymore." She started to cry again, this time silently. I wrapped her in a hug, my cheek getting wet against hers. Why was Trent doing this? Couldn't he see his marriage, his wife, was more important right now? This was not the time to go running scared. Portland was clearly vulnerable, and him leaving her to fend for herself was not fair.

"I'm so sorry, Port. That's not fair of him to do." I thought for a moment. "Have you thought about traveling with him? Maybe it wouldn't be a bad idea to just get away for awhile. And then you could be together, too."

Portland paled, shaking her head vehemently. "It's also not fair of me to give up my life to be his sidekick. He's not meeting me halfway on anything. I don't want to sound like a spoiled child, but we're supposed to a team. And he's not being a team player."

"So what do you even do? How do you go about it?" I had never given divorce a thought. It sounded exhausting. Where to start, how does it end?

"Well, I've gotten a divorce lawyer. Laura Wigstin."

"Wow. You've already gotten that far."

Portland nodded. "I'm sorry I've cancelled plans and not been around as much. That's what I've been doing, and I've just been a train wreck since hiring her and moving forward."

"But, Port, I told you. Come to me for anything. You're always welcome here. No judgments, no nothing. You're family."

"Oh, B. I feel – I feel like a failure. I've failed at marriage. And I know you don't believe in divorce and thought maybe you would want me to try harder and I just can't. I can't keep trying, being the only one putting the time and effort in. Trent acts like he doesn't even care if I'm around anyway. It breaks my heart every day that my best friend could turn his back so fast on me. Betray me like this!"

"The most important part at the end of the day is that you are happy. Do I want you to get a divorce? No. Not because I don't believe in it or that I see it as failure, but because it makes me so sad that you are so sad. It makes me angry that Trent is doing this. You are both our friends. This isn't a happy situation. But you can still always come to me. Always."

Portland sniffed and nodded. "I'm a shitty friend."

"Aw, come on. You are not. I get it, P. I honestly do. I can't say what I would have done if I were in your situation, but I very well could have done the same. This is tough, Port. Divorce isn't easy. But I want you to know we are here for you. To talk to, to lean on, to vent to. If you need a place to stay. Any packing. Any researching.

Anything. You come to us. Got it?" I didn't mean for my voice to sound like a schoolteacher, but that's how it came out.

Portland hesitated for a moment, looking like she wanted to say more. At the last moment she closed her mouth and just nodded, reaching forward for another hug. My heart sank. She was still holding something back. She still didn't trust me with something. An affair? Hers or his? How long had problems at home been happening? What wasn't she telling me?

We talked a while about the divorce and how one even happened. Portland stuttered her way through explanations and often seemed to try to draw me off topic, making me question her even more. What was she hiding about her divorce?

ॐ

Later that evening, Portland helped me whip up spaghetti for dinner while Emmy Jo ran underfoot, in a tizzy about seeing her Aunt Portland.

"Are you going to spend the night?" Emmy Jo asked, hugging one of Portland's legs while she stood at the stove, browning the meat.

"Yes, sweetie. I sure am."

"Can we watch *Tangled* and will you let me brush your hair? Maybe if I brush it, it will grow even longer and then you can toss it out the window!"

"Is *Tangled* a knock off of Rapunzel?" Portland asked me under her breath.

I nodded, a smile on my face. Emmy Jo had become obsessed with the movie lately. She couldn't wait for Halloween. Two guesses on who she was going to be.

I had pulled Aaron aside briefly once he got home with Emmy Jo and explained in very short detail what was going on. He had been appropriately shocked, asking me questions that I didn't know how to answer. I advised him to stay quiet on the D-topic unless Portland brought it up herself.

Dinner that night was awkward. I kept trying to catch myself when I used terms of endearment for Aaron, such as sweetie and babe, and I knew he was trying to do the same. I didn't realize how awkward it would be around a friend who was going through a divorce. We were trying to act like everything was normal, but I didn't want to flaunt my happy marriage in her face.

"Do you ladies have any big plans for tomorrow?" Aaron asked about halfway through the meal, munching on a bite of salad I had hastily put together.

"I think I'll come to the store and help out with inventory. Hopefully we can knock it out faster with the two of us on it," Portland said, glancing at me.

I nodded. "That would be pretty amazing. It's been slow going just getting started on it because I dread it so much. It will definitely be easier with you there."

"Trent won't be back in town until Thursday. Maybe Thursday night I can stay with you?" she asked tentatively, her gaze sliding to Aaron. He looked down at his plate, seemingly fascinated by the noodles.

"That would be great!" I said, maybe a tad too brightly.

She smiled and the table fell silent again. It wasn't until after dinner was over and Emmy Jo was playing with her toys in the living room did Portland speak up again.

"Um, Aaron? Did Brynne let you know what's going on?"

Aaron looked at me first before straightening his shoulders and giving Portland a hug. "Just a little. I'm so sorry, Portland. Trent's a stupid, stupid man."

I watched my best friend and husband embrace, and tears

pooled in my eyes. He was such a good man. He always knew the right things to say, the right action to take. I thought Trent had done the same for Portland. How could I have been so wrong? Why didn't I see any of the signs?

Portland pulled away, but then reached back and kissed Aaron on the cheek. "You have a good wife. Don't let her get away."

Aaron hugged her again, looking at me quizzically. I just shrugged, not sure what she meant by that statement. It was sweet of her to think about us, but I wasn't positive what that had to do with her divorce.

After I put Emmy Jo to bed (a bit early but she didn't seem to mind, I think Portland wore her out) the three of us gathered again in the kitchen, and Aaron poured Portland and myself a glass of wine and grabbed a beer for himself out of the fridge.

Portland explained to Aaron what she told me, and her story sounded smoother this time. No hiccups or stall tactics. He asked a few questions but didn't pry much, and I felt more at ease. Maybe she wasn't hiding something. Of course telling the story of how you and your husband are divorcing for the first time wasn't going to be easy. What had I been thinking, immediately distrusting her?

CHAPTER 16

Portland

Why didn't I tell Brynne the whole story? The drugs, the prison time Laura Wigstin was pushing for Trent. The fact that I was speaking to an agent with the Drug Enforcement Administration, who apparently had been keeping tabs on my husband for months now and was backing the said prison sentence. The incident that happened last week. I don't know. I just wasn't ready to share it all. I wasn't ready to watch Brynne's happy vision of me and Trent shatter into pieces. It was a big step and took all my willpower just to tell her I had filed for divorce. I saw the light go out in her eyes. Brynne didn't believe in divorce. She believed in partnership for life. But why wouldn't she? She had the perfect husband.

I roved around my empty house that Wednesday, packing a bag for the following night. I knew Trent would be gone again come Saturday, so I only needed to spend two nights at Brynne's house. I had a suitcase of clothes packed up, including lounge clothes to work out and sleep in. I entered my bathroom next and packed up my cosmetics, moisturizers, face cleansers. Luckily I had an oversized makeup bag that housed everything just fine.

I exited our master bedroom and strolled down the hallway to the kitchen. I opened the fridge and took out a container of blueberries I purchased a few days prior. Sitting on the island, I opened the folder containing the divorce documents. I re-read all the papers my lawyer had prepared for me and heaving a deep breath, signed and initialed where it was indicated. I would drop them off at her office in the morning, and then someone would serve Trent his divorce papers once he was back in town.

It was really happening. I was getting a divorce. Two years of marriage, done. Just like that. A simple signature ended things. I closed the folder and put my head down on the cool granite surface. No tears came. I was completely dehydrated from crying for weeks on end.

I popped another blueberry in my mouth, then scooped up the folder and headed down the hallway towards the bedroom again. I paused just before the threshold, running my fingers over the dent in the wall.

In all the years I had known Trent and been his wife, I had never once seen him become violent or out of line. At anything – least of all me. But that all changed last week. We were fighting once again, now a common occurrence in our household. I just wanted Trent to admit to me what he was doing, so we could try to figure out how to get him out of it and put that in the past. I didn't want to lose my husband, my best friend. I didn't want to be divorced at twenty-five. I was willing to look past it if he would just get help, just get out of it. But he wouldn't budge. He wouldn't tell me anything. And when I pried too hard, he snapped.

"You don't understand, Portland. I'm doing this for us. I'm working these crazy hours and traveling forty hours a week for us. Our family. I'm doing it so you can have your fancy spa days and nice clothes and manicured hands. You would think a husband wouldn't get so tortured over trying to give his wife a life that others would kill for!" he had bellowed last Monday, as I grilled him about his upcoming work schedule and complained that he was leaving again.

"Why can't you get it through your head that I don't need that life? I don't care to have the best things or take nice trips or blah blah blah! I want my husband to be home. I want my husband to be with me!" I had shouted back.

"Are you going to bring up an affair again? I don't know what the hell else I can do to convince you that there is no other woman, Portland. Call my employees, call my managers. Sure it would be downright embarrassing being checked up on, but who gives a fuck? Do it!"

"You're not listening to anything I'm saying. You never fucking listen to me! I don't want you to travel so much. I don't want to quit my job at EJs. I don't want to turn into some warped version of a housewife that shoots up with Botox during lunch hour. I want a normal freaking life with a normal freaking husband! Fuck!"

Trent had whirled around, and I saw the crazed look in his eyes. I backed up until I was just beyond the doorway to the bedroom, suddenly scared. "What the fuck do you want then?" he had hissed. "Huh? Because I'm doing what I can. I'm providing. I'm making the mortgage payments. I'm making the cell phone payments. The car payments. I provide the insurance. What the fuck more do you want from me, Portland?"

My back was pressed against the wall, and his face was right against mine. My heart was thumping loudly, but I didn't want to back down. I couldn't back down. I had to fight, fight for Trent, fight for our marriage. Fight for myself.

"Stop." That one word came out controlled and measured. My voice didn't shake. "Stop what you're doing. Please, Trent."

Something shifted in his eyes. Fear. Guilt. Shame. He knew. He knew I knew. I didn't have to say the words aloud but my little plea, the intensity in my sentence, made him understand. He was caught.

Trent looked down at the carpet beneath our feet. He looked

back up. I was so hopeful, standing there vulnerable, looking at my husband. I really thought he would sweep me off my feet, tell me he had lost his mind these last few months, and then we could move on. Call it a bad chapter and move on. But no.

His hand slapped my face so hard I could feel it in my teeth. I screamed, stunned. I had never been hit before. No previous assaults, not even a girl fight in college. My stomach flipped and I wanted to heave right there. I closed my eyes as the tears came pouring out, a hand going to my face. I could feel the sting.

His fist came next but instead of meeting my face, he crushed it into the wall behind me. When he pulled it away I could see his knuckles bleeding. I couldn't look him in the eye. My husband, a drug dealer and now abuser.

"I don't know what you're talking about," he whispered in my ear, his face next to mine again.

I had shuddered, completely disgusted that he was close to my body. Close to me. Who was this man?

"And you don't know what you're talking about either."

He had stalked into the bedroom and slammed the door behind him. I stood frozen in my spot, not knowing what to do. Run? Find a hotel? Call Brynne? There was no way I could sleep with him tonight, not a chance in hell. Was he dangerous? Would he hit me again? Was I safe in my own home?

I chose to spend the night in the basement, sleeping in the guest bedroom downstairs. By the time I had crept up the stairs close to noon the following day, Trent was gone. He hadn't left a note, but his overnight bag that was usually kept in the same spot in our walk-in closet was gone, as was his shaving kit from the bathroom cabinet. He wasn't supposed to leave again until Wednesday, but I assumed he took off early. And that was fine by me.

I was still on pins and needles the rest of the day, jumping at every noise, worrying he was coming back. I called Laura Wigstin that day and filled her in on the latest development.

"Portland, I think you need to get out of there. If Trent does indeed know that you know, he should be considered dangerous."

I had tucked my cell phone under my chin, thinking about her words. "I'm not scared, Laura. I think the slap was a one-off, honestly. He's never been abusive before. And now he's gone again until next week, so I'll be fine. If I need somewhere to go next week I'll try my friend Brynne. But I'll be okay."

Only, it wasn't okay. Trent came home late Sunday night, crawling into our bed around four in the morning. He reeked of booze, sweat – and something else. Drugs? Another woman? I couldn't be sure, I just knew something was amiss. I was on my stomach, my favorite sleeping position, trying my hardest to will myself to sleep, to at least keep my breathing steady. Trent touched a cold foot to my leg. I didn't move. He touched me again; I continued to ignore him. Luckily he passed out quickly. But the next morning when I confronted him, he slapped me once again. It wasn't as hard this time and he immediately started apologizing, stumbling over his words about how he was so stressed and my nagging wasn't helping anything, but I was done. I was not going to put up with abuse on top of everything else. I deserved better, especially from my husband. I had stormed out and gone straight to EJ Reads, where I knew I could find Brynne. I hadn't planned on collapsing in a sobbing heap on the floor, and I was thankful no other customers were around to see my breakdown. How humiliating.

I knew Brynne would take me in with no questions asked, but I just couldn't bring myself to bare it all to her. She would be devastated to hear about the drugs, the abuse, and I just couldn't do that to her. She was under enough stress as it was with her pre-cancer and doctor appointments and running the store. She didn't need my added baggage. I would tell her the rest of the story once her next results came back clean. Her mind would be lighter. It would be better.

ℬ℘

Lucy,

It's been great being able to email you and stay connected. Are you still planning on coming up for Thanksgiving? I wish it weren't so far away! Maybe I should plan another trip to New York. That might not be out of the question. Things have taken a turn for the worse with Trent. I won't bore you with too many details but things have actually gotten...violent. Don't worry, nothing awful. Just a slap or two. Barely felt it. It's really nothing terrible, I promise. And before you ask, yes, my lawyer is aware and she is trying to get me to move out. But with Trent gone all the time, I don't see why I should have to give up my home and impose on Brynne. Not that I think she would care in the slightest, but you can only take so many sympathy hugs and awkward conversations. I'm sorry, I'm probably boring you. What's new on your horizon? How was your photo shoot the other day? If you didn't snap a pic with Blake Lively I'm not sure we can keep in contact. JK(Kinda). Talk soon!

Portland

ℬ℘

"Port! Great news!" Brynne opened the front door of her home and rushed into my arms. I hugged her back, not sure what was causing my friend's happiness.

"What is it, B? You're killing me!"

"Got my latest test results – all clear!" Her green eyes were positively sparkling, and she had a rosy glow to her cheeks.

"Oh, Brynne! That's terrific news – but I'm not surprised. Six more months to go, two more tests, and you can put this whole debacle behind you."

She hugged me again. "I was at lunch with Aaron when I got the call. He's insisting on celebrating tonight. I think that means he's bringing home dinner. You'll stay won't you? You must celebrate with us!"

"Of course I'll stay. I can't tell you how happy I am for you. I knew you could beat this." And I did. Of course Brynne would beat pre-cancer, to not even let cancer invade her body. I pushed down the surge of envy, completely inappropriate for a friend to have. I was happy for Brynne. Of course I was.

"Yay, thank you!"

"What should we do until then? How about a good pedicure? My treat!"

Brynne giggled happily and soon we were out the door, off to get our feet rubbed, buffed, and toenails colored. By the time we got home (after our short trip to the bakery to toast Brynne's good news with red velvet cupcakes) Aaron and Emmy Jo were home.

"And there is my beautiful wife and her ever so lovely best friend!" Aaron exclaimed once we walked through the door.

Emmy Jo burst into giggles and gave us each a hug. "Daddy has been so silly today! He's in a good mood. He even bought me a new hairbrush from the grocery store!" She ran on her little legs to the couch in the living room and came back seconds later with a teal blue hairbrush in her hands. "It's a special *Tangled* brush. It will make my hair grow!" She dutifully ran the bristles through her short brown hair and smiled at us.

"That's just great, baby. Maybe you can brush our hair later, too?" Brynne said, smiling at her daughter.

She nodded solemnly. "I'll brush your hair extra long, Mommy. Portland already has long hair!"

I laughed, scooping up my goddaughter for a hug. "Mommy definitely needs my extra brushes."

The celebration dinner that night was laidback and had me feeling content. I could do the divorced thing. It wouldn't be the end of the world. The awkwardness from previous dinners with Brynne and Aaron seemed to be gone. There was no stumbling over words or asking tough questions. Each day was getting a little better. The pain was starting to lessen. My friends were supporting me. Life was going to be okay.

I laid in bed that night thinking about how to tell Brynne the whole story about my failed marriage. I knew she was going to be devastated to learn about Trent. Like Brynne said not all that long ago, Trent was one of their best friends. He went on trips with them. Brynne and Aaron confided in him. He was the godfather to their daughter. He wasn't just betraying me, he was betraying his friends as well. If he had family, his family would be horrified (I was sure) in the path he chose to take.

I tried to work through my feelings that night. I couldn't take blame for Trent deciding to get into the drug business. From what I could piece together over the last few months, I think Trent just got sucked into living in a grand world, and he needed a quick way to get it. I wish he would have talked to me. I didn't need the flashy life, the big house, the expensive car. Was it nice to have? Sure. Was it necessary? Not even in the slightest. I just wanted a normal life. A loving husband. Maybe even a kid or two down the road. Why didn't Trent want the same? Why did he let such superficial fantasies invade his life – and ruin it?

I turned over, the tears running down my face. I was trying my hardest to accept it, to move on. But he was my husband, my best friend. My other half. And he threw it all away for what? A bigger bank account?

My chest started to rise and fall rapidly. I needed to get a handle on my emotions. Crying myself to sleep every night wasn't helping anyone, especially not me. I hated being exhausted each morning, having to pack on the concealer under my eyes when doing my makeup. I just needed to calm down. Life would go on.

℘ᴂ

Dear Lucy,

That picture was about the most amazing thing EVER! I'm going to print it out and make you autograph it. You are rolling with the big wigs now, and I know real soon you'll be working your way up that fashion ladder. Good thing Darlene hooked up with my dad so I can now have someone famous in the family! Can you get me tickets to New York Fashion Week? I've always wanted to go! ;)

To answer your last question, my mom named me. I've asked my dad the story about my name too, and when I was in high school he finally gave me the truthful version. It's not that cool. Embarrassing really. Mom was dabbling in drugs before she was pregnant (probably also in the very early weeks of the pregnancy) but she and Dad were so happy to be expecting that she decided to give rehab another chance, to stay clean while carrying me. She went to rehab in – you guessed it – Portland, Maine. She told Dad that it was the best rehab stay she had experienced (um, yay?) and while she was still all crazy from the hormones, epidural, and pushing me out of her body, she told the nurse she wanted to name me Portland. So yes, I am named after a rehab stint. Insert the awwwwww moment, right?

That's just my life I guess. Thanks again for listening to me babble away night after night. I'm so grateful we made this connection. Good night!

Portland

ℬ Ϙ

When I was young, my mom passed away. She chose drugs over her life. She chose drugs over her husband and daughter. Entering my parent's bedroom that October morning and seeing my mom lifeless was the worst moment in my life. I will never forget the look of her eyes – still open. I won't forget her arms that were stretched on either side of her with the palms up, like she was reaching out for me even after passing. I won't forget the sinking feeling in my little body knowing instinctively my mom was dead.

Death weighed on my mind greatly after that day. I almost became morbid myself, constantly thinking about death, how people died, when it was their time to die. When would my dad die? My teachers or neighborhood friends? When would I die?

ℬ Ϙ

Lucy,

Please tell my dad I am so, so sorry. And please tell Brynne I didn't mean to keep secrets from her. I thought I was doing the right thing. Please tell them I love them. Please tell———

MESSAGE SENT

CHAPTER 17

Brynne

My life is good. I have a loving family who has supported me in every decision from what to wear for school pictures to leaving college early and getting married young. My husband is the perfect match for me. We have a beautiful and healthy daughter that makes me so unbelievably happy and filled with love that sometimes it physically hurts. I have my own business and get to do what I love every day. If I had to rack my brain and think of the worst memory in my twenty five years of living, I can only come up with one. One bad memory. Oh sure, I got a bad haircut (bowl cut to be precise) in the seventh grade, I almost failed a simple accounting course in college, and my florist was late on my wedding day – but I'm talking real bad memories. Serious stuff.

My worst memory comes from the beach when I was about nine years old. We were having a family day, just me, Mom, and Dad, and the sun was shining and the sand was hot. I wandered to the shoreline by myself, as I had done many times before. I squinted my eyes towards the water and saw a pink bucket floating amongst the waves, and decided I must have it. It didn't look too far, so I started treading water to get to it. I realized after a while that I was actively swimming towards it, but I still couldn't seem to reach it. Before I knew it, my feet were no longer touching anything and I was swimming with the waves, chasing the pink bucket. I could hear yelling from the shore and when I looked back, my mom and dad were screaming at me and waving their arms. I realized then how far I had swum. Panic started to grip me, and I tried to paddle my way to safety. A huge wave came and captured me, taking me out further away from my parents. I started screaming for help; I had never been that far out before. My dad had jumped in the water and was swimming toward me. I tried my hardest to reach him, but my arms got too tired to go further. When I woke up I was on the sand again, throwing up water. I almost drowned that day going after a pink bucket.

I can remember the utter panic I felt as a nine year old girl, the feeling of the waves dragging me farther and farther away from my family and safety. When I really think hard, I can remember the moment where I gave up. When I knew my little body couldn't keep swimming, couldn't keep treading water. When I couldn't hold my head above water or hold my breath any longer, and knew I had to succumb. I could hear the waves roaring in my ears. I could see the black spots appear before my eyes. I take a deep breath...and all goes to black.

∽⅋

"Brynne? Brynne, baby! What's happened? Officer, what is going on?"

I come to on the bench in our entryway. My head in Aaron's lap; his blue eyes filled with concern and fear.

"What – what happened?" I mumbled, blinking rapidly to try to get my bearings. Did I faint? Why was a police officer – Officer Ryan Hepling to be exact – in my home?

"I'm so sorry for the shock, Mrs. Ropert," Ryan said, his young face still unlined from all the hardships his job would undoubtedly bring him in time.

I sat up, feeling my head whoosh. "What?" I asked again.

Aaron laced his hand through mine as Officer Hepling opened his mouth once again. "I'm so sorry to bring the news, but Mrs. Portland Dolish has been found murdered in her home. We've called her father and he is on his way to Delany. We – the community – know how close you are. We wanted to give you the news in person."

My heart squeezed. My eyes became heavy with tears. My body went limp against Aaron. No. What? No. Not Portland. What? This officer was insane. Delusional. No. What?

I heard Aaron clear his throat over the roaring in my ears. "I'm sorry, Officer, but this is a complete shock. Portland – our Portland – is dead?" His voice hitched on the last word. I turned my face to look at him. He was pale, tears in his eyes. I could see the confusion, the pain, the horror, that I was sure reflected in my own eyes.

What the hell was going on?

"We received an anonymous call that someone was needed at the Dolish location. Upon arrival we found the victim, Portland, deceased."

My mind swam in all different directions. Portland couldn't be dead. And murdered? Who in the world would murder my best friend?"

"Who?" I whispered. "Who did this?"

"No one was at the home when we got there. We've called her husband and he is upstate on business. He's also on his way down."

"So who did this? Who did this to her?" I didn't realize my words had turned into screams.

Aaron wrapped his arms around me and folded me into him, his hands on my head like he was trying to cover my ears, not wanting me to hear any more of the details.

I sobbed into his chest, still not able to comprehend how my life was just shattered. My best friend was ripped away from me too soon. How was this possible?

I heard Officer Hepling start talking. Words like "strangulation" and "deceased for two days" made me gag. I didn't make it to the hallway bathroom before the vomiting started. I sank down on the tiles and heaved, again and again and again. All I could think of was *no, please. Please not Portland. She doesn't deserve this. She doesn't deserve this.*

Officer Helping said they had some suspects in mind, but couldn't give out that information yet. But apparently another house out in the country had recently been burglarized, so there was a possibility that a burglar thought Portland wasn't home and she confronted him or her or them. They also were trying to track down the location of the anonymous phone call to see who called the tip in. I got sick again thinking about Portland losing her life because some random person wanted to rob her. How did that make any sense?

After the officer left, Aaron went downstairs to check on Emmy Jo who was napping, and I fell onto the couch, not sure what the hell I was supposed to do. Make phone calls? Go to Portland's house? Fall apart? Falling apart won. I sobbed uncontrollably, crying so hard I started heaving again. I didn't have anything else left in my body to throw up so I just dry heaved, my throat burning, tears hot on my cheeks.

I flashed back to the last time I had seen Portland, just two days ago. *Two days ago.* Office Hepling had said she had been dead for two days. Was I the last person to see my friend alive? I started shaking and couldn't stop. This couldn't be real. This couldn't be happening to us. This was a movie script, not real life. Murder didn't happen in a town like Delany. Crime was barely an issue here.

"Honey? Honey!" Aaron was walking up the stairs and rushed

over to me, seeing that I was shaking like a leaf and seemingly unable to stop. He wrapped me in a blanket and held me. After a few moments, it registered that he was crying.

I tilted my head up to look at him, not used to seeing my big strong husband crying. "I'm sorry. I was trying to keep it together. But – what the fuck? How could this happen?"

I shook my head. "I hurt so bad, yet I feel numb. I don't know how this is possible. What do we do? Where do we start? Do we call someone? Trent? Jim? Start making a – arrangements?" I could barely say the word. Portland's funeral. I was going to have to plan my best friends' funeral.

"I have no idea, baby. I have no idea. I just – I just want to hold you a little longer. I love you, Brynne. I love you so much."

I burst into tears again and tucked myself into Aaron. While I was experiencing shock and disbelief, Aaron was feeling fear. He was seeing how fast someone could be pulled from your life.

A short time later, we both went down to Emmy Jo's room. She was awake in her bed, and she asked us if we would watch *Tangled* with her. Without a word, we jumped in on either side of her. I put my arm around her little body and breathed in her scent, never wanting to take having my daughter in my life for granted.

ʕ♡ʔ

My once nice, stable, sometimes boring life suddenly flipped a page, and chaos abounded. Chaos – and extreme sadness. Jim and Darlene were at our home that night. When I got the call from Darlene, Aaron and I were still in Emmy Jo's bed. It was like we were trying to savor the last few moments of calm before the storm we knew would hit landed. But once the phone rang I immediately sprang into action, having Aaron call his parents and asking them to take Emmy Jo overnight. With word getting out, our house was surely about to be a focal point with the community, and it was no place for a three year old to be.

Jim and Darlene were the first to arrive. The pain etched into Jim's face was nearly unbearable. We embraced, and I had no words to say. I just hugged him as I tight as I could, and offered him coffee and a cold sandwich that I had thought to whip up.

Darlene was a little more vocal, and she was the one taking charge. "We've been talking to the police over the phone on our drive up here. Someone is going to be coming here at seven to give us an update on the investigation. They had people over there taking pictures and dusting for fingerprints. They're going to find this guy. There will be justice. There just has to be."

Around five, the company and phone calls started pouring in. It seemed everyone from the town was either calling with their condolences or stopping by the house to offer hugs, comfort, or food. Our kitchen countertop was soon overflowing with casserole dishes and takeout bags. No one stayed too long, but it was clear that the town was experiencing a devastating loss.

Mr. Jones and his wife were one of the first to stop by. Mr. Jones, a regular at EJ Reads, looked forlorn as he gave me a hug. "She was a great girl," he whispered in my ear. His wife brushed tears from her eyes as she repeated the gesture.

Juliette Mabry and her husband dropped by just before Office Hepling returned. She thrust a casserole dish into my hands and then wrapped her arms around me. "I'm so sorry, Brynne. This just isn't right." She shook her head, her long red braid being tossed over her shoulder. "I hope you get some answers – and soon."

"Thank you for coming. We appreciate it." I must have spoken those words hundreds of times that night, and I was practically monotone by that point. But Juliette did look devastated, and even though I knew she helped spread rumors about Trent, I couldn't hold a grudge against her. People gossiped. People told stories. But nobody expected murder in this town.

Office Hepling and a detective, Brad Vogelsong was his name, came to the door just after seven. The house was quiet, only Aaron, Jim, Darlene, and myself sitting in the kitchen, just staring into space. Aaron answered the door after the bell went off, and I immediately stood to fix the men a cup of coffee and offer them food from a plethora of options.

Officer Hepling looked exhausted, surely not used to such an investigation in Delany. Detective Vogelsong looked to be in his late fifties, with chiseled cheekbones and a shock of white hair. He was tall and broad, and loomed over the shorter Officer Hepling. I didn't recognize him, which was odd since I knew everyone in this town. He spoke first. "My name is Detective Vogelsong, and I've been assigned to this case. It is clear that this was a homicide versus a suicide." I saw Jim wince out of the corner of my eye. My heart ached. Homicide. Murder. Portland. No. "I'm going to need to take a statement from each of you regarding the personal life of Portland Dolish, when you last spoke to her or saw her, those sort of items. Who was the last one to see the victim alive?"

The four of us glanced around, and then I raised my hand as if in school. "I'm fairly certain it was me. I was at her home two days ago."

Aaron, Jim, and Darlene nodded in agreement. I had indeed been the last one to see her alive.

"Okay, I'll start with you, Mrs——?"

"Ropert. Brynne Ropert. I'm Portland's best friend and also employer. Was. I guess." I stumbled over my words, still not sure how any of this was real. This couldn't be happening. Portland would walk through the door any minute. She had to.

"All right. Do you have a room we could use for privacy?"

"Yes." We exited the kitchen and I showed him to the master bedroom. I perched on the bed while he took a seat on my vanity, notebook in hand. "Do you mind if I record you also?"

"No, that will be fine." It crossed through my mind then that I might be considered a suspect. Should I have a lawyer with me? "Do I need my attorney?"

"I don't think that will be necessary. I just want to find out a few more things about Portland, including the last time you saw her. You aren't under suspicion, Mrs. Ropert."

I relaxed slightly. Heaven forbid anyone would think I killed my own best friend.

"Okay. Let's get started. Can you state your full name, phone number, and address please?"

I recited them off, then fell silent again.

"And what is your relation to Portland Dolish?"

"Friend and employer."

"What is the name and address of your company?"

I gave the address for EJs.

"When was the last time you saw Portland Dolish?"

"On Sunday, two days ago. I was at her home."

"And was Portland acting unusual?"

"Not that I noticed, no."

"Are there valuables in the home of Portland Dolish?"

"Yes. They have multiple large TVs, several computers and laptops, and both Portland and her husband have an iPad. Portland also has jewelry in the home that is worth a lot, and I know they have some expensive paintings in their basement." I paused for a moment. "And they have a safe as well that they keep papers, passports, and some money in."

"Do you know where the safe is located?"

"Yes."

"Do you know the combination to the safe?"

"Yes."

"Who else would know the combination to the safe?"

"I suspect just Trent."

"How is the relationship between Trent and Portland?"

Another pause. My mind whirled. Portland was filing for divorce. Do I say that? "Portland was in the process of filing for a divorce."

I assumed this wasn't news to him, as he only nodded his head. "When did you become aware of this?"

"Just a few weeks ago. Portland was filing for divorce and using Laura Wigstin as her attorney. When I spoke with her two days ago, she had just signed the papers and Trent was going to be served shortly." My heartbeat sped up. Oh my God. Trent. I hadn't even considered him. Did Trent kill Portland – over a divorce? No, that couldn't be right. But the hair on my arms slowly rose.

"Did you think it was unusual not to hear from Portland since Sunday?"

"No. She was supposed to work on Monday at the store, but she asked me Sunday if it would be all right if she took off. She wanted to start packing, because she was going to move in here with us temporarily while the divorce was happening. I offered to help but she said it was something she wanted to do on her own. I called her this morning from the store, wanting to check in on how she was and if she needed my help yet moving the boxes. I really didn't think anything of it when she didn't answer. I just thought – I thought she would just call me back later."

The detective gave me a few moments to compose myself, before starting up the questioning again. "Do you know why Portland was seeking a divorce?"

I rubbed my arms. "Trent travels a lot for work. She was getting tired of him always being gone, and she said he didn't seem to care about her anymore or making their marriage work. She was unhappy, and didn't feel he was being a team player." Those were Portland's exact words.

"Did Portland seem afraid of her husband?"

I thought hard. "No. Not at all. She was just fed up with being second best to his career. Trent is our friend, Detective. If Aaron or myself ever thought anything was going on in the home, we would have gotten Portland out of there and gotten help for Trent. I don't think he's your guy."

ଫ ଉ

As the clock neared midnight, the questioning from the detective finally slowed. Both Office Hepling and Detective Vogelsong left for the night, but said they would be back in the morning. I followed them to the door. "Can I ask a question before you go?" I said, just as they were about to slip out the door.

"Go ahead," Office Hepling said.

"Where is Trent? We've tried calling him a few times but it's going to straight to voicemail. I know you mentioned he was on his way to Delany from up north and I just assumed he would come here..."

The officer and Detective exchanged a glance. "We won't have more information for you until probably tomorrow, but Mr. Dolish is down at the station right now for questioning."

"You don't think he could have done this, do you?" Aaron questioned, coming up behind me.

"We can't answer that right now. But in homicide cases, the spouse is almost always looked at first." Officer Hepling patted my shoulder. "Get some rest, Brynne, Aaron. I hope to have some more answers for you tomorrow."

We stumbled back into the kitchen, where Darlene and Jim were still perched in the chairs at the table. Jim stood when I entered and held out his arms. I fell into him, this man being like a second father to me. He had lost his wife in tragedy and now his daughter. What he had to have been feeling I couldn't even come close to imagining. He hadn't cried all day, but now he openly wept. Darlene wiped her face with his hanky, and even Aaron teared up once again. I had seen my husband cry more today than in all of our years together – including a pre-cancer diagnosis and the birth of Emmy Jo. Everything about this day was just wrong and unsettling.

"I'm so sorry, Jim. I'm so terribly sorry," I whispered.

The four of us sat at the table, silence taking over. What were we supposed to do now? All of my actions felt foreign and downright weird. How could I eat when Portland was dead? How could I smile when my best friend had been strangled to death? How could I take my makeup off and brush my teeth knowing I would never see her again? I just wanted to curl up into a little ball and make it all stop.

"I'm going to try Lucy again. She's been in Paris the past few days for work and hard to reach, but I know she and Portland were forming a friendship. She'll want to come home," Darlene said, pushing back her chair. She dropped a kiss on Jim's head before heading to the deck.

We were still sitting in silence when the door opened moments later and Darlene stepped through. "Still no answer. I'll try her again in the morning. Jim, let's get to bed, yes? We'll need our strength for tomorrow."

Jim nodded and slowly stood. I approached him, wrapping my arms around his sturdy frame and burying my head into his chest. I didn't cry this time. I just wanted to give comfort and feel comfort. Jim kissed my cheek when we pulled away, then allowed Darlene to take him by the hand and lead them to our guest room.

Aaron blew out the candles we had lit at the kitchen table and reached for my hand. Silently, just like Jim and Darlene before us, we exited the room.

CHAPTER 18

Brynne

I woke up Wednesday morning cuddled next to Aaron. I lifted my head and realized I had a pounding headache. Looking at the clock, I saw it was 8:32. I startled. Where was Emmy Jo? She was usually up by now and running into our bed, begging for breakfast or to let us let her brush our morning breath away. I threw the covers off and jumped out – when it all came rushing back. Office Hepling. Portland. Dead. Murder.

"No!" I screamed, sinking back into the bed. Aaron awoke with a start, by my side in a flash.

"Brynne, it's going to be okay. It's going to be okay. I got you, babe. It's going to be okay."

I sobbed into his chest, the inane thought of *oh, my tears are back, I guess I'm not dehydrated* running through my mind. Who thinks that when their best friend is dead? How fucked up am I?

ౠ ౠ

Tuesday night was the worst night of my life. Wednesday morning was the worst morning of my life. People from the community started coming by around ten. Officer Hepling and Detective Vogelsong returned just after lunch. Jim hardly spoke to anyone. He kept going out onto the deck and just staring at the sky, as if he was trying to see his daughter in heaven. Darlene bustled around, putting away the casserole dishes and organizing the take-out boxes, talking to people in hushed voices, and answering the incessant phone calls. I wouldn't realize it until later, but she was really the glue that kept everything together. Aaron tried hard, but it seemed he was walking around in a daze as well.

Just after lunch, where I could do nothing more than pick at a cold sandwich, Detective Vogelsong walked through the door and asked to speak to Darlene in private. I looked up in confusion. Why would he need to talk to Darlene? He took her statement last night like he did the rest of us. Why would Darlene need to be the one he speaks to in private first? Oh my God, was it Darlene? Could Darlene have killed Portland? What was her reasoning? Jealousy of Portland and Jims' relationship? I was coming to love Darlene. I couldn't imagine her strangling——

"What's going on, Detective? What's the meaning of this?" Jim asked gruffly, coming up behind Darlene and laying a hand on her shoulder.

"We've been trying to get in touch with your daughter, a Miss Lucy Eckstrand?"

Lucy killed Portland? She killed her then fled to Paris?

"She's in Paris for work," Darlene said, her eyes wary.

"If we can just maybe step into the bedroom for a moment." Detective Vogelsong cut his eyes to me, and my back stiffened. What did he need to know about Lucy that couldn't be said in front of me?

Darlene nodded and the two disappeared. Jim paced the floor, Aaron cracked his knuckles, and I stared out the window. This was getting ridiculous. I had to stop thinking that every name mentioned was a possible killer. It was a burglary gone wrong. It was probably some punk kid that got scared. It wouldn't be anyone from our community, it wouldn't be a family member. I had to get a grip on myself.

Darlene and the detective returned about ten minutes later, and with a few terse words he was out the door again. Darlene sat at the table, her face etched in confusion.

"What was that all about? Everything okay?" Jim asked, sitting next to his partner.

"He said it was all right if I told you," Darlene said, clasping her hands. "Portland and Lucy had taken up an email relationship. They emailed almost every night. They – they were getting so close." Her voice hitched, and she brushed a tear away. "The police seized all the computers, laptops, and iPads that were in the house last night. This means that burglary is ruled out. Nothing was taken from the home." My mind could barely register that sentence. I had been so sure it was a burglar. What did that mean?

"They were able to get into Portland's emails. It seems that – that Portland and Trent's marriage was in trouble. Perhaps more trouble than she let on." She looked up at me then.

"I told the detective she filed for divorce. Trent was being served late last week." I was still confused. I knew that. Portland didn't keep secrets from me.

"She mentioned in her emails some – some physical altercations."

"What?" I shrieked. "Trent was physical with her? When? Why? Why wouldn't she tell me that?" Oh my God, it was Trent. Trent killed his own wife. "What did he do to her?"

"She said it was just a slap. That was her words. Just a slap. But her last few emails to Lucy has the police worried. When they were talking to Trent last night he denied ever having touched her. The emails prove differently."

"Trent? No way. He loves Portland. He wouldn't hurt her. Right, Brynne?"

Aaron was looking at me with the familiar horror in his eyes. When did we get thrust into a Lifetime movie? When would it end?

"There's more." Darlene spoke before I could comfort my husband. My heart twisted.

"Trent's alibi isn't stacking up. He claimed to be in Petosi all day Sunday, but his manager there said he didn't get in until almost eleven. They have cards to get into the gym after a certain hour, and Trent's card wasn't used until that time. They don't have all the – the results back yet, but it looks like Port – Portland passed away probably in the morning on Sunday."

I put my head in my hands. My thoughts were swimming. Why was Trent lying? Was he scared? Or...or did he do it?

"I – I don't understand. Portland never said anything about physical abuse. I swear to you, Jim, if I knew I would have pulled her out of that house so fast. I––"

"I know, Brynne. I know." Jim had come around and was now hugging me. "This isn't your fault, honey. Don't you worry."

Darlene spoke again. "Officer Hepling is going to be stopping by soon. He has the emails that we can see. There's some stuff in there that might clear up a few things for you, Brynne. But for now, Trent is in custody. He's being charged with murder."

ॐ

Lucy,

Sometimes this town just feels too small for me. I wish I could escape – maybe to New York? Everyone knows everyone here, knows all their business. I swear, these people probably all know what we've had for dinner and what's in our trash cans. Sorry, I hate complaining. Let's talk about something fun. Send me an email of the latest pair of shoes you bought. That will cheer me up!

Portland

Lucy,

Fab shoes, just fab. Can I use your discount sometime? I wish I could say my birthday's coming up but it's totally not. Bummer. Yes, I did go out with Brynne yesterday. We did a little shopping to blow off steam. She's doing good. She's so positive, it's rare to see her get down in the dumps. I feel bad when I complain around her because she always wants to put a positive spin on things. Sometimes I just want to get angry, you know? I don't want someone to try to fix my problems, I just want to be mad. That makes me sound like the worst kind of person, doesn't it? Eesh. Off to eat a frozen dinner.

Portland

Lucy,

Paris?! Can I come in your suitcase? Do you need like a minute-taker or photographer to come and help? I don't think things are getting any better here. I should have the divorce papers from my lawyer shortly. It feels so weird to admit failure. I'm going to be a divorcee at 25. God, that just sounds awful. How embarrassing. I haven't told Brynne yet, but I know she is going to be shocked. I hope she's not too disappointed in me. Brynne's the type that believes in happily ever afters. And she has every reason to. Aaron is her Prince Charming. I never realized when I married Trent that I was getting the frog.

Portland

Lucy,

I know you're right, Brynne deserves to know. I told her last night about the divorce. Just busted right into EJs and started crying on the floor. Dramatic much? Yikes. But of course you were right. She was nothing but supportive. What is wrong with me lately? I know you said that everything with Trent has shaken my trust, and I think you must be right. I've never been this guarded in my life, especially when it comes to Brynne. I keep realizing how badly I've been treating her and it's so unfair. She did nothing to deserve this. It's not her fault Trent has changed. I just feel so awful sometimes that I literally get sick to my stomach. Of all the people I don't want to lose it's Brynne. I have to figure out how to be a better friend.

Portland

Lucy,

You seriously always know the right things to say. Friendship is a funny thing isn't it? Especially when you've been friends for as long as Brynne and I have been. It's like we have a sister relationship now. I know I am pissing her off lately. She has this guarded look in her eyes like she never knows what's going to come out of my mouth. But then the next minute everything is fine and she is my biggest protector. I'm lucky to have her. Thanks again for always listening to me complain.

Portland

Lucy,

It's been great being able to email you and stay connected. Are you still planning on coming up for Thanksgiving? I wish it weren't so far away! Maybe I should plan another trip to New York. That might not be out of the question. Things have taken a turn for the worse with Trent. I won't bore you with too many details, but things have actually gotten...violent. Don't worry, nothing awful. Just a slap or two. Barely felt it. It's really nothing terrible, I promise. And before you ask, yes, my lawyer is aware and she is trying to get me to move out. But with Trent gone all the time, I don't see why I should have to give up my home and impose on Brynne. Not that I think she would care in the slightest, but you can only take so many sympathy hugs and awkward conversations. I'm sorry, I'm probably boring you. What's new on your horizon? How was your photo shoot the other day? If you didn't snap a pic with Blake Lively I'm not sure we can keep in contact. JK(Kinda). Talk soon!

Portland

Lucy,

I understand what you're saying, but please don't worry about me. I really don't think Trent meant to slap me. I truly think he's harmless. I know he's upset about the divorce. I mean, it's divorce. It's not a happy time. Emotions are high. If I ever don't feel safe I know to go to Brynne's. She's been a rock of course. I think things are finally on the right path with her again. I'm working up the nerve to tell her about the slap. And the hole in the wall. I know once I do she'll basically forbid me to stay in the house. I just don't see why I have to be the one to get out. Trent's doing this. It's his fault. So I have to give up my beautiful house and my space and my comfort? It's not fair. Here I go complaining again. How do you handle my emails? I must bring you down. You're just like your mom. As much as I didn't want to like Darlene at first (I guess I was just weirded out by Dad dating), it was impossible. Within the first two minutes of meeting her I knew she was a keeper for Dad. Tell me a little more about what it was like growing up. Where did you go to high school? Did you do any activities – cheerleading, yearbook? Let's talk about YOU

Portland

Lucy,

Thank you so much for those HILARIOUS pictures! I would not have recognized either you or Darlene, and actually had trouble believing they were really you for a minute! Oh, high school was the days, huh? Trent will be home Saturday and then he's not leaving again until Monday. The divorce papers were served today. He's been blowing up my phone like crazy but I have yet to respond. It's all in there, besides of course the DEA being after him. I can't say anything yet until they do the bust or raid or whatever you call it. I'm going to head to Brynne's. Divorce sucks a big one.

Portland

Lucy,

I did not see this coming. This might sound really stupid and over dramatic, but save these emails okay?

Portland

Lucy,

Please tell my dad I am so, so sorry. And please tell Brynne I didn't mean to keep secrets from her. I thought I was doing the right thing. Please tell them I love them. Please tell———
MESSAGE SENT

ൠ

My whole body was trembling once I got done reading all the emails Portland sent to Lucy. I didn't know whether to feel hurt, furious, sick, devastated, confused...I guess I was all of them. How could she go to Lucy – a virtual stranger – with all her problems over me, her friend of nearly a decade? I knew that sometimes it was hard for us to talk about deeper issues, but this was a life or death situation. She was in danger. Did she not realize it? Didn't she trust me? She talked about trust issues in one email, but why would she trust Lucy over me? None of this made sense. And now Portland was dead and I couldn't even ask her about it.

My mind still couldn't seem to make sense of it. I accompanied Jim to the funeral home to help pick out her casket and to see the spot where she would be buried. Next to her mother, back in Sweeney. Delany would be hosting her wake and services, then only immediate family (and us of course) would attend the funeral on Sunday. I went through her closet to pick out the dress she would be buried in. She always loved her satin white dress, the one that made her feel like Marilyn Monroe. I told the director at the funeral home not to put too much makeup on her, and to leave her blonde hair down and flowing. That was her favorite hairstyle.

I picked out a pearl necklace for her to be buried in, one that she didn't wear often but I knew was special to her. Jim gave it to her when she graduated college and she wore it on special occasions. When I showed Jim, he had to leave the room because the tears started.

The crying seemed to hit us at the weirdest times. Neither of us cried when we went to identify the body. We went together and held hands while we said good-bye in private, but the tears didn't fall. Can you believe we had to confirm the body was Portland? Even the guy at the morgue knew it was Portland; Delany is not that big of a town. But for whatever policy they had in place, they needed a family member to confirm it was indeed Portland Laurie Dolish lying on a cold, sterile bed. They had a sheet covering her all the way up to her neck. I didn't realize it until after we left, but I was positive it was covering the bruises on her neck. From Trent. Her husband. My husband's best friend. My friend. I was friends with a murderer. Oh my God. Emmy Jo's godfather was a murderer.

Aaron and I had a closed session with Detective Vogelsong just one day after Darlene told us he was being charged with murder. We turned over any emails we had from both Portland and Trent, grabbed cell phone records including text messages from the two, and gave official statements that could possibly be used in court against Trent. We also both agreed to take the witness stand if necessary. Me. On a witness stand. In a murder trial. Unthinkable.

I had asked if we could speak to Trent while he was being held. I wanted to look my friend in the eye and feel it in my gut that he did not kill his wife. Detective Vogelsong said Trent was refusing to see anyone at this time other than his attorney. That cowardly move made me even more sure he had done it. The bastard took my best friend away from me. The evidence was slowly mounting against him. He would surely do prison time because of his drug-distributing business, which the DEA had enough evidence to hold him accountable to, but a murder charge would put him away for life. Maine didn't support capital punishment, so he wouldn't even get the easy pass to Hell. He could rot in his cell the rest of his life. That bastard.

"Aaron! Oh my God, Aaron. Aaron!"

"Brynne! Brynne, are you okay? Brynne!"

I was sitting straight up in bed, the covers thrown off me and my eyes looking around wildly. Aaron rushed into the bedroom and launched himself onto the bed.

"What happened? What's wrong? What happened?" He looked absolutely terrified.

"Trent. Trent is Emmy Jo's godfather. Her *godfather*, Aaron. He signed her baptismal certificate. We have to get a new one made. We can't – we can't – we can't." I was sobbing now, heaving sobs. Our life was so fucked up. Nothing would ever be normal again. My best friend dead. Our friend a murderer. Emmy Jo's godfather behind bars. Her godmother set to be buried in the ground tomorrow. How could we explain this to Emmy Jo when she was older? How did anyone move forward from this?

Aaron stroked my hair until I cried myself to sleep.

ℬ℧

I awoke in the morning at five, unable to find sleep again. I drug myself to the bathroom, apprehensively looking in the mirror. I looked like hell. My skin was sallow, my dark hair greasy and matted around my head, and my eyes seemed sunk into my face.

I leaned against the sink and took a deep breath. I did not want to cry anymore. I was tired of crying. Tears weren't helping the situation. My parents had Emmy Jo last night and today because I was too afraid of falling apart in front of her. I had to pull myself together at some point. I had to try to figure out how in the world to find normal again in our lives.

But I gave myself one more day before I would let that happen. The wake and funeral planned for today were going to be hell to get through. Jim and I were both giving eulogies. I had to be able to speak on behalf of my best friend.

I took a shower and blow-dried my hair once I finished toweling off. I put my sweat pants and T-shirt back on, preferring to wait until the last minute to put on my black dress. Mom had bought me the dress yesterday, as I knew I would only want to wear it this one time and then donate it. It would only make me remember the pain of this day if I kept it around.

Speaking of my mom, around eight I heard the garage door opening and knew it would be her. Sure enough, she walked in carrying a casserole dish and a jug of orange juice.

"Let me grab that." I rushed to her from my perch on the couch and grabbed the orange juice. We walked into the kitchen, where she peeled the lid off the dish and grabbed a spatula from the drawer.

"It's just an egg bake, and it should only need a few minutes in the oven to get warm. Is Aaron awake?"

"Yeah, I heard the shower running a few minutes ago. He should be here anytime."

She opened the oven door and slipped the dish inside. "You ready for today?"

"Is anyone ever ready for this day? I'm just hoping it goes by fast and I don't retain memories," I said, which was pretty much the truth. If Portland's funeral could just be wiped from my mind I wouldn't complain.

"Have you heard anything further on Trent?"

"It's pretty bad, Mom."

She took a seat next to me. "What do you mean? What's happened?"

"That detective that I told you I didn't recognize – Detective Vogelsong? He's from the Drug Enforcement Administration, and had been tailing Trent for a while now."

"The DEA?" Mom looked baffled. "Whatever for?"

I took a deep breath, right as Aaron entered the room. His blue eyes seemed glazed over, as if he still couldn't believe the news we were delivered last night.

I turned back to Mom. "Trent has been involved in a drug-distributing business for the past year. The employees that he hires helps him buy and sell the drugs, and they have been using the gyms as a cover for it. He's responsible for young kids getting their hands on drugs like cocaine. One girl even died in the town that was hit hardest – Petosi."My voice faltered, and I thought about Juliette Mabry and how she had tried to tell me. I brushed her off as being a gossip. If only I had taken her seriously, maybe I could have warned Portland...and she would still be alive. "They had been tracking Trent and his people for months now, and were just about ready to bust them. He'll be charged with all sorts of illegal activity, but now he's also being charged with Portland's murder, even though he still claims it wasn't him. From the emails that were found it seems Portland figured out what was going on, and the police speculate she confronted Trent about it and he...."

Aaron let out a choked sob, and I had to scrunch my nose up to try to keep my millionth tear from falling since I heard the news run down my face.

"We had heard the rumors that Trent was dealing drugs. We dismissed them, because we thought we knew our friend. We thought it was ridiculous. I can't believe we thought so wrong. I can't believe that Portland didn't get the hell out once she knew. What was she thinking? A drug dealer? I don't understand." I fell silent again, simply repeating everything I had said last night to Aaron, Jim, Darlene, and Lucy, who arrived late Thursday night with a pale face and runny nose. I knew it was childish, but it was hard to look at her. My best friend had trusted her over me. I just kept thinking that maybe if I knew what Lucy did, I could have saved her.

"I don't know if it will ever make sense. I would have never of thought this of Trent. I truly don't think he's a – a sociopath. I think he just fell into something and got in too deep. But why kill Portland – that will never make sense. His own wife. I will never understand," Aaron said, grabbing a tissue. It was still so strange to see my tough husband being brought to tears.

Mom sat in silence, her head bowed down. I picked at a hangnail, barely noticing when my finger started to bleed. Our lives had flipped completely. Someone I thought I knew, who I trusted to be in my house and with my daughter, was leading a horrific double life. And my poor friend had gotten caught up in it, and lost her life because of it. It didn't matter to me if Trent killed her or if he had one of his guys do it, he was still responsible for this. My heart was shattered into so many pieces I wasn't sure it could ever be whole again.

CHAPTER 19

Brynne

September

"Brynne? It's time for you."

I moved my head just inches to the left, indicating I had heard my mother. I stared into the mirror, taking in my black dress with a hint of a bubble skirt, the string of pearls around my neck, and my red lips. Portland was always going on about the importance of lipstick, though I hardly ever wore any.

"Brynne? Everyone is waiting." I finally turned away from my reflection, meeting my mother's eyes. She squeezed my hand and slipped the index card with my speech on it into my sweaty palm. "You'll be just fine, darling. You can do it."

I nodded, feeling my brown bob graze my neck and then brush away. I walked out of the small room with my mom, entering the large area where everyone awaited to hear me speak. I took my place, my hand shaking as I looked at the index card. I looked over the sea of people, everyone from our small town there supporting Portland. I looked at my best friend next, taking in her flowing blonde hair, her smooth skin that never seemed to find a blemish or a sunburn, even when we stayed on the beach for hours. Her white dress didn't clash with her fair skin or light hair, it just made her look like she was glowing.

I cleared my throat. "Portland Dolish is my best friend." I looked over at her once more, tears filling my eyes. "I was lucky and fortunate to be paired with her as roommates in college. We were soul sisters from day one, and for the last few years of my life, it was like we were blood sisters. Portland had the biggest heart, was always willing to help, to listen, to console. I chose her to be godmother to my daughter, not because she was my best friend, but because I knew she would relish her role. She would teach my daughter right from wrong and she would be a loving support throughout her life. Portland was not only a friend and godmother, but a loving daughter. She cared for her father so deeply, and family was important to her. I am so grateful that she considered me family, and so blessed to have so many wonderful years with her by my side." I was full on crying now, but kept pushing through. "It doesn't seem right that we have to say goodbye today. It isn't right that such a lovely person, soul, was taken from us too soon. But I hope we can remember Portland's spirit for what is was. And may her memory live on."

I took my seat after giving Jim a hug, who spoke his eulogy next. I'm sad to say I have no idea what he said. I buried my face in my hands once I was seated and continued to cry. Aaron and my mom flanked my sides and helped keep me upright. I was thankful for that, afraid I would have just melted into a puddle on the floor in their absence.

After the services were over, a meal was being served at The Window for the community. We went for about thirty minutes, not eating, but just saying thank you to everyone who had been supportive over the last few days. I couldn't handle eating a full meal, nor could I handle being in a room where light chit-chat was being had and people were smiling. They could move on. I wasn't there yet.

Emmy Jo had been starting to ask questions about Portland, and I had no idea what to tell her. How do you explain death to a three year old? How could I tell her that her Aunt Portland would never come back? That we wouldn't be able to make her favorite brownies anymore, or have Port come with us to the ocean?

The first time, just two days after we were told the news, we were eating a silent dinner at the table, just the three of us. I couldn't manage to make a meal yet, so we were simply eating a leftover casserole that was dropped off from someone around town. Emmy Jo broke the silence, asking, "Is Aunt Portland coming tonight?"

I felt terrible, but I nearly choked on my piece of chicken and had to run out of the room. I didn't know how it hadn't crossed my mind yet that EJ would be sure to have questions, and I hadn't prepared myself for them yet. I was sorry to leave Aaron to field her query, but I just couldn't face it yet. I just couldn't.

Two nights before the wake and funeral I was tucking Emmy Jo into bed, talking about how she would stay with her grandparents the following night. "Why do I keep staying with Grandma and Grandpa? Are you sad, mommy?"

I didn't have the convenience to run away that night, as Aaron was in the shower and it was just me and my daughter.

"Oh, baby. Mommy's all right. Me and Daddy have something important to do tomorrow, that's all. A grown up thing."

Emmy Jo looked at me with serious green eyes. "Will Aunt Portland be there? Will you tell her I want to brush her hair again? I think the *Tangled* brush is working!"

My eyes filled up with tears again, and I started to smooth back EJ's fine hair, trying to find the courage for this conversation. "Portland – Portland won't be there. I'm sorry, honey, but Portland is...gone."

"Well, where did she go?"

"She's – well, baby, she's in Heaven."

"Heaven? Where angels are?"

"That's right. She's our own angel in Heaven now. So even though we won't see her again, she'll watch over us every day."

"She's not gone, Mommy. I saw her before I went to bed last night."

The hair on my arms rose. "What do you mean? What did you see?"

"I saw her by my door before I could fall asleep. I said her name, but then she was gone."

My lips trembled. Did I believe in ghosts? Had Emmy Jo really seen her, or was she perhaps dreaming?

"Like I said, she's our angel now. She's always watching over us, and sometimes you might think you see her and that's okay. That's great." The tears were falling freely now, and I tried my hardest to brush them away. I didn't want to frighten Emmy Jo.

"Next time I see her I'll ask her to cheer you up, mommy."

That was the end of our conversation. I could only nod my head, give her another kiss, and then quietly exit her room, her words weighing heavily on my mind.

Aaron and I talked in length about what Emmy Jo could have possibly seen. We chalked it up to a dream and an active imagination. But sometimes, when I'm feeling really lonely and missing my best friend, I like to imagine that she really is our guardian angel, keeping watch over Emmy Jo. It makes my heart feel lighter.

The weeks and months passed achingly slow for me. I let Serena and Aaron's mom work at the store more, the memories of Portland held inside those walls too much for me to handle at the moment. I did my best with Emmy Jo, really throwing myself into her activities and daycare projects, always volunteering to be a room or field trip mom. It was awkward around town at first, because it seemed no one knew what to say to me. The talk was rampant after the funeral, everyone wondering what would happen to Trent when the court case finally started happening. Even the national news came to our small town, and the story was run in magazines and newspapers from around the country. How could a seemingly normal man with a good and happy life turn out to be a drug-dealing murderer? No one could make sense of it. But the town of Delany really banded together after Portland's death. The support my family received was tremendous, and we even started a foundation in Portland's name. Our goal is to raise awareness about drugs, get into schools and talk to kids, and to even start a scholarship fund for our local children to help them with college.

I'll always wonder why Portland didn't tell me the truth about Trent and her marriage. I'll always wonder if I wasn't good enough in some way for her to tell me the story. But I'll always keep her memory alive, the one that I chose to remember. The days where our bond never seemed tighter, the times we would finish each other sentence's like an old married couple, her smile that could light up a dark room. I didn't want to remember Portland as someone who was sad, stuck, and afraid. And even though I told my mom I would rather not know who killed my best friend, that question continues to haunt me after we laid Portland to rest. Could Trent have possibly murdered his own wife? Did he hire someone to do the deed for him? And how could justice ever be served?

EPILOGUE

Portland

I've made a lot of mistakes in my life. Not studying for tests, breaking hearts, getting into fights with my dad. Dying my hair brown (which turned it gray) volunteering to be a flyer in cheerleading (I hate heights), and starting an oven fire on a disastrous Thanksgiving Day four years ago when I decided to cook because Brynne was pregnant. But the biggest mistake of my life? Not understanding how dangerous my husband was, and not getting out when I knew I should have.

It's easy to look back now and see that Trent was a completely different man from whom I married. It's easy to see that I should have been honest with Brynne, so she would have pulled me from that house by my hair if necessary to ensure I was safe. But I kept everything hidden inside. I was embarrassed, and that embarrassment only made the whole situation worse.

It pains me to watch Brynne, the sadness she feels, the guilt that emanates off her. I want to wrap my arms around her and tell her it was all my fault. I was stupid and foolish. I was acting like a high school girl, wanting my friends to believe my relationship with the football captain was so stellar, when really he was making out with another girl behind the bleachers after fourth period.

I was able to watch my funeral, which nearly killed me all over again. Brynne did such a good job picking out my outfit, telling people how I wanted my hair and makeup to look. I looked almost normal again. Except that I was dead.

I do believe my life ended too short. I know people say God works in mysterious ways and only He knows when it's your time to go, but I'm sorry, I don't believe it was mine. I had so many years ahead of me, so much to see, to do, to learn. The only upside that I can see right now is that I'm with my mom, and we have a relationship once again. She's with me up here to help me get my bearings, help me come to grips with the fact that my life on Earth is over. She tells me how she can watch over people below at times, how she can even help and interfere from time to time. When I asked why she didn't watch over me the night of my murder, she just shook her head and shimmied from the room. Did that mean she didn't want to? Or couldn't? I'm still not sure where our limits begin and end yet. But I plan on taking my godmother duties just as seriously up here, and will watch over Emmy Jo as often as I can.

I don't think Trent meant to kill me. He would go on to be charged with premeditated murder after the police found some emails that counted as evidence against him and he eventually confessed to my murder, and will serve life in prison. I should have realized the night he was home that he was under the influence of cocaine, but I was still too naïve to think my husband dabbled in the drugs. I wanted to believe he was only selling them. Our argument was heated; he kept insisting that he was doing it for us and just wanted us to have a better life. Why he couldn't understand that wasn't the life I wanted still isn't clear to me. Why wouldn't he listen to me? At one point I slapped him right across the face, for all the pain and hurt he had caused me. My marriage was over because of his decisions, because he wouldn't listen to my pleas. He slapped me back; I threw our framed wedding photo at his head, just barely missing him. If only

Mom could have intervened and let me nail him, maybe the night would have had a different outcome.

But I only seemed to enrage him, and before I could think of running for help, he had both hands around my throat and was quite literally squeezing the life out of me. The last thought that ran through my mind as everything turned fuzzy and then to black while looking into my husband's eyes, was how disappointed I could imagine everyone would be. I was going to be a statistic. I was going to be known as the wife of a druggie, who was killed her in their own home. The daughter of a druggie, the wife of a druggie.

I don't know if it was the drugs or just not wanting to believe it, but Trent hightailed it out of the house once I passed out. I know now that he repeatedly called our home and my cell phone, like he thought I was going to answer, that he didn't leave me for dead on our living room floor. On the carpet that we had picked out together for our dream home. He was the one who finally called the tip in to the police, so my body would be discovered. I'm just thankful Brynne didn't come over since it had been two days since we had last spoken. If she would have been the one to find my body – I just can't even go there. And to think if she had Emmy Jo with her? That would have been unimaginable.

I'm done feeling sorry for myself up here. I've learned to let all that go. I spend my time talking with Mom, watching Earth, and trying to protect Emmy Jo. I've found a new peace that I never experienced in my life before. Who knows? Maybe there was a reason for Him to take me. Maybe I would have never found peace or happiness in my life. That thought makes me sad, but there is nothing I can do about it now. I can only continue to learn, to grow, and to help. Mom said something to me about getting an assignment, where I can help someone on Earth that is in the same situation that I was. I guess that's a part of what we do up here. We don't just roam around and be lazy and eat grapes. I'm glad to have a purpose, and I'm ready to get my assignments once They decide I'm ready. I will work harder than I ever did in my life to help other women not become like me. Something tells me this is the reason I'm here, the reason why I was taken. When I think about that, a peace spreads over me.

I can see Emmy Jo now from up here. Brynne is dropping her off at daycare before heading to her latest Pap test. I hope the results come back clean. I wish I could figure out how to intervene with that, to make sure the cancer stays far away. But as long as I can keep watch on EJ, I'll be happy. I owe it to Brynne. I understand now, with my newfound clarity up here, that Brynne was always willing to listen to me and my problems. Even though I assumed she lived in this perfect bubble, I can see now she doesn't. She should have been the person I went to, she could have helped save me. I guess over the years we had somewhat of a questionable friendship – carefree and caring from the outside, but when we tried to dig deeper, we got stuck. That makes me immensely sad, not only for me, but especially for her. She deserved more than what I could give her.

But I know now that I can't change the past. I'm dead, I'm in Heaven, and now I can only watch and try to offer my guidance from up here. And I know there will never be a question about that.

ACKNOWLEDGEMENTS

I can't imagine writing books without my never-ending support group. Thank you to my family for always cheering me on and especially to my mother for all the hard work you put into this book. To be able to work with you on my manuscript was such a special experience. Thank you to my new husband for always encouraging me and letting me talk his ear of about anything and everything writing and publishing. To my new family, who as always treated me as one of their own. My friends are an amazing support group, and I thank them for letting me bombard them with snap chats along the way. Thank you to my beta readers, Kaley Stewart, Kayla Paine and Ashley Byland, and another thank you to Cat Lavoie and Laura Chapman. I absolutely adore working with ladies. To all the Chick Lit Plus supporters, again, thank you so much for the never-ending support and encouragement I receive when I turn on my computer. It really is mind-blowing. And finally to my grandmother. Book three, can you believe it? I miss you.

AUTHOR BIO

Samantha March is an author, editor, publisher, blogger, and all around book lover. She runs the popular book/women's lifestyle blog ChickLitPlus, which keeps her bookshelf stocked with the latest reads and up to date on all things health, fitness, fashion, and celebrity related. In 2011 she launched her independent publishing company Marching Ink and has three published novels – Destined to Fail, The Green Ticket and A Questionable Friendship. When she isn't reading, writing, or blogging, you can find her cheering for the Green Bay Packers. Samantha lives in Iowa with her husband and Vizsla puppy.

If you enjoyed this book you'll also enjoy...

Destined to Fail
Zoey & The Moment of Zen
Breaking the Rules
The Green Ticket
Hard Hats and Doormats

CPSIA information can be obtained
at www.ICGtesting.com
Printed in the USA
LVHW021457190319
611158LV00020B/1893/P